"What if the police say that there is no reason to provide protection?" Rochelle asked.

Again, Matthew wondered exactly what she was up against. She looked as though she might cry. Compassion flooded through him. "We'll cross that bridge when we get to it. I'll stay with you now. You need to focus on your recovery."

She looked up at him for a long moment, probably trying to figure out why he was going to all this trouble. "Can I have your phone, so I can call my son? I need to know that he's okay."

He placed the phone in her hand. "Everything is going to be all right. I'll see to it that you get well so you can take care of that kid of yours. It would help if you told me why these men are after you."

Matthew heard the ___ ___ ___ The blow to the back ___ ___ ___ in his brain.

The last thing ___ ___ ___ collided with the floor was Roche ___ ___ ned scream.

Books by Sharon Dunn

Love Inspired Suspense

Dead Ringer
Night Prey
Her Guardian
Broken Trust
Zero Visibility
Guard Duty
Montana Standoff
Top Secret Identity
Wilderness Target
Cold Case Justice

SHARON DUNN

has always loved writing, but didn't decide to write for publication until she was expecting her first baby. Pregnancy makes you do crazy things. Three kids, many articles and two mystery series later, she still hasn't found her sanity. Her books have won awards, including a Book of the Year award from American Christian Fiction Writers. She was also a finalist for an *RT Book Review*s Inspirational Book of the Year Award.

Sharon has performed in theater and church productions, has degrees in film production and history, and worked for many years as a college tutor and instructor. Despite the fact that her résumé looks as if she couldn't decide what she wanted to be when she grew up, all the education and experience have played a part in helping her write good stories.

When she isn't writing or taking her kids to activities, she reads, plays board games and contemplates organizing her closet. You can reach Sharon through her website, www.sharondunnbooks.net.

COLD CASE
JUSTICE

SHARON DUNN

HARLEQUIN® LOVE INSPIRED® SUSPENSE

Recycling programs
for this product may
not exist in your area.

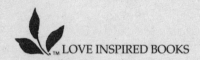

™ LOVE INSPIRED BOOKS

ISBN-13: 978-0-373-44638-4

Cold Case Justice

Copyright © 2014 by Sharon Dunn

Printed in U.S.A.

For I am the Lord, your God,
who takes hold of your right hand and says to you,
Do not fear; I will help you.
— *Isaiah* 41:13

This book is dedicated to all the women and men
who work tirelessly to help teen moms
have a fighting chance in life.

ONE

Rochelle Miller stopped dead in her tracks when she spotted Elwood Corben across the wide corridor of the courthouse where she worked. She took in a deep breath to clear her head as her anxiety level skyrocketed. Why, after ten years, had the man she'd fled Seattle over shown up in Montana? It couldn't be coincidence. Elwood Corben had hunted her down. But why now, after all this time?

Elwood was speaking to a police officer, their heads bent close together in a very cozy way. She thought to slip into a room before he saw her, but fear paralyzed her. Elwood caught her staring, grinned at her and walked across the corridor. Each of his footsteps seemed to crush her further into the floor.

His face was all teeth and narrow snakelike eyes. His dyed hair couldn't hide that he was a man past sixty. "Megan, how good to see you."

Even changing her first and last name hadn't kept him away. He must have hired a detective to find her. She'd thought she'd been careful in covering her tracks, but she'd been only sixteen when she'd run from him and hadn't had the resources or know-how to do a thorough job in changing her identity.

Rochelle laced her fingers together to hide how badly they were shaking. Though Elwood Corben wouldn't harm her with all these people around, she'd picked up on the threat beneath his words. Only she knew the truth about Elwood Corben—that he was a cold-blooded murderer.

She squared her shoulders and purged her voice of the terror raging inside her. "I have to go to work." She hurried toward a courtroom that she knew had just adjourned. She slipped into the milling crowd and headed toward a side exit. When she looked over her shoulder, she couldn't see Elwood among the throng of people. Working her way through the labyrinth of the courthouse, she took a circuitous route to the side street where her car was parked. The winter cold chilled her skin as she got into her car. She hadn't had time to get her coat or her purse, but was glad she had shoved her keys into her pants pocket. Her heart raced as she slipped in behind the wheel and started the car.

Her only clear thought was of her nine-year-old son, Jamie.

When she pulled out, Rochelle checked her rearview mirror to make sure she wasn't being followed. She tried to formulate a plan as she drew closer to Jamie's school. Corben knew where she worked, but maybe he didn't know where she lived. Why else would he have come to the courthouse instead of her home? She'd hidden away cash at her house in case this day ever came. First she'd get Jamie and then the money. Rochelle feathered the brake as she turned a corner onto a busy street, knowing she needed to slow down or she'd end up on the sidewalk.

She wove through the heavy traffic. Her car fish-tailed on the icy road. A horn honked. She gripped the wheel a little tighter. For sure, Corben didn't know about Jamie, and he wasn't going to find out. Yet another reason to get out of town quickly and not go to the police. If she lingered here in Discovery, even if the police could protect her, Corben would find out he had a grandson. She couldn't take that chance. Elwood wasn't capable of loving family members. She knew that all too well.

Rochelle tensed as the images from ten years ago assaulted her mind.

She'd only been sixteen when she'd fallen in love with Corben's son Dylan. Though Elwood Corben walked around with a smoldering rage, she hadn't understood the extent to which he was involved in illegal activity until she heard Dylan arguing with his father one night. Dylan insisted he was not going be a part of the family's import/export business because his father often operated outside the law.

She'd come to the balcony of Elwood's house and listened to the heated discussion.

Dylan's voice held conviction. "I want a legitimate life, Dad. I want to marry Megan."

The silence that followed caused her to hold her breath. From her vantage point she saw only Dylan's back and part of Elwood's arms and upper body.

"You are my son and you will do what I say."

The barely contained rage in Elwood's words made her shiver. She saw Elwood's fist swing out and strike Dylan, who crumpled to the floor after hitting his head on the counter. She could have viewed Dylan's fall as an accident brought on by Elwood's out-of-control anger, for Elwood hadn't known Dylan would hit his head. But as she watched Elwood stare down at his son and do nothing, she saw him for the murderer he was.

Blood spread across the tile. In the moment that life left Dylan's body, something died inside her, too. Though she'd been in rebellion from her Christian upbringing when she met Dylan, she had loved him.

She must have screamed, because Elwood stomped across the tile and glared up at her where she stood on the stairs. Murder glistened in his eyes. "What did you see?"

She shook her head, unable to stop staring at Dylan lying motionless on the floor. Knowing that Elwood intended to kill her for what she'd witnessed, she'd fled from the house. He'd caught up with her before she could get to the police station, threatened her life and her family's. She'd managed to escape his grasp and taken the first bus out of town. Two days later, when she'd made it to Discovery, she found out she was pregnant. Up until that point, she had intended to go back and talk to the police. Once Jamie was born, though, she knew she had to protect him from Elwood ever finding out he existed. Elwood would hardly be the doting grandfather. If Dylan had been any indication at all, Elwood sought only to control family. When he couldn't control, he killed. She couldn't risk Jamie being a party to that.

Not wanting her family to be harmed or Corben strong-arming them into saying where she was, she'd cut off contact with them, as well.

Rochelle stared through the windshield at the icy road as her heart pounded out a wild rhythm. Her arm muscles tensed as she gripped the wheel. She was less than two minutes away from Jamie's school. She pressed the accelerator and swerved around a slow-moving car.

The car that hit her came out of nowhere. She didn't even have time to touch the brake before she heard the crunching of metal. Her body swung back and then forward. Glass sprayed across her field of vision.

As her world went black, all she could think about was holding her nine-year-old son and making sure he was safe.

Paramedic Matthew Stewart felt a tightening in his stomach as the sirens of the ambulance he was driving wailed. He maneuvered around the stopped traffic.

His partner, Daniel, leaned forward in the passenger seat as they got closer to the scene of the accident. "This doesn't look good."

Up ahead, Matthew could see that a truck with a dented passenger-side door had been pulled to the side of the road. A compact car with a crumpled front end sat in the middle of the street.

His neck muscles tensed.

This was the first serious call he'd been out on since Christina Johnson's suicide, and his adrenaline was mixing with his anxiety. A neighbor had phoned that he'd found Christina unconscious with a broken ankle. When she came to, she said she'd fainted and twisted her ankle when she fell. The ER doctors had signed off on her after they patched her up. But Matthew's instinct had told him something more was going on. Yet, he'd done nothing about it. Christina hadn't acted like a suicidal woman. No one thought to question her fainting story. A week later, they were called back to her house. This time, she'd taken enough pills to kill an elephant, not just pass out and fall down. He couldn't sleep at night because he kept going over and over in his head why he hadn't trusted his gut, and he vowed next time he would.

As the crowd of gawkers parted, he killed the siren and parked the ambulance. He pushed open the door and grabbed the C-collar and the backboard from the back bay. An older man ran up to him.

"The guy in the truck is okay." The man pointed at a twenty-something man who was rubbing his neck. "The woman is in real bad shape, though." The older man indicated the compact car.

Daniel patted Matthew's shoulder. "I'll have a look at him and then come help you."

Matthew drew his attention toward the car in the middle of the street. The front end had been completely pushed in and the windshield had been smashed. He couldn't tell the condition of the driver from this far away. In the distance, he heard the sound of the police sirens headed toward them.

As he stepped toward the car, he saw the woman's head rested against the driver's-side window. He opened the door slowly and began his assessment. Despite the winter chill, she wasn't wearing a coat and her eyes were open but unfocused. Blood dripped from the gash on her forehead. She was pretty, probably in her late twenties. She looked vaguely familiar to him.

He knelt and spoke softly. "Ma'am, you've been in an accident."

She shook her head. The glazed eyes told him she still wasn't tracking with him. "I have to get to the school…for my son. Please…I have…to leave town."

Why was she thinking about leaving town? Not a normal response for an accident victim. She wasn't making much sense. She might have a head injury. "Ma'am, can you tell me what day it is?"

She met his gaze. A light came into her eyes. "Do I know you?"

He studied her more closely. "I think we might be neighbors. Do you live on B Street?" He'd seen her playing in the yard with her son and getting in her car in the morning dressed in a business suit. He'd talked to the kid a couple of times and knew his name was Jamie.

"Yes, just up the street from you." She nodded. Pain shot across her expression, compressing her features. She moaned. "My arm."

He touched her shoulder. "Please don't try to move. My partner and I are going to put you on a backboard and get a collar around you to prevent any additional injury to your spine."

"I don't need to go to the hospital." Her voice filled with panic. "I can't. Please, I have to get my son." She arched her back and closed her eyes, probably trying to shut out the pain.

Even without a close exam, he knew her injuries were extensive. Though she was free to refuse medical attention, she clearly needed it. He didn't want a repeat of what had happened with Christina Johnson. He had to convince her.

"What's your name, ma'am?"

"Rochelle."

"Rochelle, I'm Matthew. I can appreciate that you are concerned about your son. We'll make arrangements for you to call a friend to pick him up. But right now, my priority is to get you to a hospital."

She shook her head. "You don't understand." She swung out of the car seat and attempted to push herself to her feet. He caught her before she collapsed to the ground. Her eyes opened briefly and then she became a rag doll in his arms.

"I got it," said Daniel as he ran toward them, grabbing Rochelle's legs and helping Matthew transfer her to the board.

She stirred only slightly when they strapped her to the backboard and put the collar around her neck. The crowd dispersed as they loaded her into the ambulance.

"I'm going to ride in back with her," said Matthew.

While Daniel moved into the flow of traffic, Matthew started an IV. They passed a tow truck headed in the opposite direction. Up front, he could hear Daniel calling ahead to alert the hospital of their arrival.

Matthew stared down at the porcelain-skinned brunette. He had said hello to her once or twice when he went for a walk in the evening. His house was a few houses down from hers and on the opposite side of the street. He'd talked to the kid several times. He felt a connection to the boy when he'd seen him in the yard trying to learn how to throw a football. Matthew's father had left the family when he was seven. No one had been there to teach him to throw a football, either.

Her eyes fluttered open briefly. "Jamie." The note of desperation surprised him. Nothing he said seemed to calm her down.

"I know that's your son. I've talked to him a couple of times. Nice kid."

She didn't respond.

"Rochelle, you've got glass in the cut on your forehead. I'm going pull it out and put a bandage on you."

She turned her head to one side, eyes closed. "My arm hurts, and here." She touched her rib cage.

"I've got an IV going for the pain. We'll have a doctor look at you as soon as we get to the hospital." He hadn't seen any sign of external bleeding other than her head, but there was no telling what kind of internal damage she'd sustained.

"I have to go. I have to get out of here. Please." She wrapped her arm around his bicep and squeezed before her voice faded, and she closed her eyes.

What was going on in her life that she could not let go of the idea that she had to leave? He hoped the kid was okay and that her worry was being fueled by the trauma of the accident. He found tweezers and carefully picked out the pieces of glass. She winced each time. He disinfected the wound and placed a bandage over the gash.

She looked up at him with wide brown eyes. He locked into her gaze for a moment. Though he had only seen her at a distance, he'd always thought she was pretty. She turned her head to the side and closed her eyes. "I have to call someone to go get Jamie." Fear lanced through her words.

At least she seemed to be tracking with reality and had given up the idea that she had to get her son. He studied her for a moment wondering exactly what her story was. His concern for the kid's safety heightened.

The ambulance pulled up to the ER doors. The trauma team met them outside with a gurney.

As they were wheeling Rochelle inside, Matthew tapped the nurse's shoulder. "Marie, when this woman is stabilized, can you make sure she has access to a phone? She's concerned about her son and needs to make arrangements for him to be picked up. I'm not sure what's going on."

Marie nodded. "We can take care of that."

He watched them push the gurney down the hall and disappear around a corner. Matthew finished out his shift with only one minor call. With Rochelle and her son still on his mind, he swung by the nurses' station before leaving for home.

An older, plus-size nurse with brassy hair and pink lipstick sat at the station flipping through a patient chart.

"Lindy, there was a woman brought in from a car accident earlier. Did she get access to a phone?"

Lindy crossed her ample arms. "She did, as per your request, Matthew."

"How's she doing?"

"No serious internal damage. She's got bruised ribs and a fractured arm. They're keeping her overnight to make sure no latent head injury shows up." Lindy studied him for a moment. "You don't usually take this much interest in patients."

"She's a neighbor and she was emotionally distraught." His gut was telling him something more was going on with her. This time, he intended to listen to that instinct. He had to know she was going to be okay before he went home.

Lindy narrowed her eyes at him. "Didn't your supervisor suggest you take a few days off after that suicide tore you up so bad?"

"Work is the best thing for me." Honestly, sitting at home wondering what he could have done different to save Christina Johnson would only make things worse.

"You can't rescue everyone from everything. Sometimes you've just got to hang it up once your shift is over," Lindy said.

"That's not what's going on here." He sounded like he was trying to convince himself. He wasn't stepping out of bounds. He just didn't want another Christina on his hands.

Lindy shrugged. "It's your call. I'm about to do my rounds. You're welcome to pop your head in and say hello to her yourself."

He wouldn't be at peace to leave work until he saw that Rochelle was okay and that whatever panic she had at the scene had been because of the accident and not something else.

He followed Lindy down the hall. When they stepped into the room, the bed was unmade but empty. Lindy checked the bathroom and then shook her head. "Looks like our patient checked out on her own." She bustled toward the door. "I'm not sure what recourse we have for getting her back here, but I'll talk to the doctor. I hope we find her. That woman needs rest and medical supervision. She's in no condition to be running around."

Feeling a rising sense of panic, Matthew darted toward the door. "I know the first place to look for her."

TWO

Pain shot through Rochelle's bruised rib cage as the taxi pulled up to her house. Cradling her fractured arm in a sling, she leaned to the side and studied the street. She recognized all the cars as belonging to people in the neighborhood. Hopefully, she'd been right about Corben only knowing where she worked. She'd been careful through the years not to list her address publicly, instead using a PO box. How Corben had found her was anyone's guess. Something connected with her court-reporting work and a picture of her must have appeared somewhere online that a detective could track her down.

The cabdriver turned his head. "This is the place, isn't it, lady?"

"Yes." Her purse and her phone were still back at the courthouse. "Can you wait here? I'll have to go inside to get the money to pay you and then I'm going to need a ride to the airport after we pick up my son."

The taxi driver shrugged his shoulders. "It's your dime, lady."

Bracing herself against the pain, she pushed open the door and headed toward her house. She stepped with care on the icy sidewalk. At least Jamie was safe for now. The kind paramedic had kept his word and made sure she had access to a phone as soon as she was able to talk. She'd called her friend Louise to pick Jamie up from school and keep him at her house. If she had her cell phone she would have called just to make sure he was still okay.

As she made her way up her sidewalk, she could still feel the aftereffects of the painkillers she'd been given. She was groggy and weak. With one more glance up and down her street, she entered her house. Even if it was a risk, she had no choice in coming back here. She and Jamie would not survive without that money, and she needed to grab another form of ID to get on the plane.

There was no time to pack. She'd get clothes for her and Jamie later in whatever city they ended up in. After finding a ski jacket for herself, she grabbed Jamie's favorite book and then went to her own closet to dig out a shoe box filled with the money she'd saved over the years. She'd stored the cash at the bottom of her closet, knowing that this day might come. Rochelle placed the money in a fanny pack and clicked it around her waist, hiding it under her shirt. Out of breath and in intense discomfort, she sat on the floor using her bed as a backrest. Though the medication took the edge off the pain, she still felt the effects of the accident. The effort it took to kneel and find the box had exhausted her. But she had to push through. She could sleep when she was on the plane.

She hurried through the house, stopping only for a moment to grab a passport and to look at the pictures Jamie had drawn that were plastered all over the refrigerator. Deep sorrow washed over her. She'd made this place a home for her and her son. Now she'd have to say goodbye. She grabbed Jamie's drawing of a rocket ship and put it in her fanny pack. The house seemed eerily quiet as she closed the door.

Once outside, she headed down the sidewalk and toward the taxi that waited for her across the street. She'd taken only a few steps when a broad-shouldered man stepped out from behind the neighbor's hedge. The look on his face was menacing. He had a two-inch scar underneath his eye that made him look even more threatening. He lunged toward her, grabbing her good arm. She screamed. The pain as she tried to wrench away nearly made her crumple to the ground. She looked toward the taxi, but seeing the trouble, the driver sped away.

"Elwood wants to talk to you." Her attacker's gruff voice spiked the fear she felt.

With her heart pounding, she struggled to break free. White-hot pain exploded from her rib cage. The man grabbed her injured arm as black dots filled her field of vision.

As she fell to the ground, the last thing she heard was pounding footsteps.

"Get away from her." Matthew ran up and knelt on the ground beside Rochelle.

The man reeled backward, panic evident in his expression as he stared down at Rochelle. "I barely touched her."

"This woman is injured. She needs to be in a hospital." Matthew pulled out his phone.

"You calling the cops?"

He glared at the man. "You assaulted her."

The thug shook his head, turned and ran down the

street. Matthew returned his attention to Rochelle. He'd deal with getting the police onto that guy later. His primary concern was for Rochelle. As he gathered her into his arms, her eyes fluttered open.

"I know that something terrible must be going on for you to leave the hospital when you did," he said. "But you make your injuries worse by running around like this."

She nodded as though she understood and then closed her eyes. He laid her gently on the grass and ran to get his car. After pulling up to the curb, he gathered her into his arms and positioned her in the passenger seat. She stirred slightly when he reached over and belted her in.

"You don't understand." Her voice was groggy. "I have to leave now." Even in her weakened state, he heard the determination in her voice.

"You're too weak to go anywhere, Rochelle." She still hadn't let go of that idea. Judging from the behavior of the man who had come after her, she was in some danger. Still, the best place for her was the hospital. He'd call the police and see if he could get their help. As he drove, he phoned the hospital to let them know he'd found the missing patient and was coming in.

Maybe if he knew what was going on, the police would be more likely to help. "Who was that guy anyway? An ex-husband or something?"

She opened her eyes and stared straight ahead. "I wish it were that simple." Anguish colored her words.

Daniel met them at the door with a wheelchair. Rochelle got into the wheelchair without much protest.

"She was in room 112. I'll go down to the Admitting and make sure her paperwork is still in place," Matthew said.

"Got it," said Daniel.

Once inside, Daniel pushed the wheelchair in the opposite direction that Matthew went. Matthew made his way down the hall and turned the corner where the admitting desk was. A muscular blond man stood at the high counter. Matthew couldn't hear all of the hushed conversation, but he heard Rochelle's name. The administrator clicked the keys on her computer and responded to the man.

Something about the man was just as menacing as the one with the scar on his face, the man who had attacked Rochelle in front of her house.

Trust your gut.

With adrenaline surging through his veins, Matthew turned and ran back down the hall.

When he looked into room 112, it was empty. They must have assigned her a new room. At least that bought her some time. He had no idea what kind of threat Rochelle was under or who the men were. He only knew he wanted her to have a chance to recover from her injuries. He scanned the hallway wondering where Daniel would have taken her. When he glanced over his shoulder, the blond thug stalked down the hallway toward room 112. The paperwork must still say she was in that room.

Matthew ran toward the nurses' station. Lindy was no longer on duty. Instead, a perky young nurse named Tina smiled up at him.

"Did Daniel the EMT come by here with a woman in a wheelchair?"

"He turned her over to the nurse to get her settled in room 125." Tina pointed down the hallway.

"Thanks, Tina." Matthew glanced over his shoulder.

Blondie came out of room 112 and made a beeline toward the nurses' station, stopping to glance into the rooms with open doors.

Matthew hurried down the hall and opened the door to room 125. Rochelle was pushing herself out of the wheelchair, reaching for the wall for support. She lifted her head. She looked more coherent than she had previously, though her face was still pale.

"Where's the nurse?"

"She went to get some medical supplies. Matthew, I know you're only trying to help me, but I need to go."

"I agree with you."

A look of surprise and confusion crossed her features as she shook her head.

"You've got company in this hospital," he said.

Her eyes grew wide. "They found me already." Fear made her voice falter. She shot toward the door, then stopped, swaying slightly.

"Unfortunately, I think I led them here. I told that guy at your house you needed to be in a hospital. He must have phoned his muscular friend. Get back in the chair." This was his fault. He needed to make it right. "He's checking the rooms. Let's move you to a safe place and then we'll call the police and get some help for you."

"I'm not sure if the police can help." She wobbled and reached out for the wall.

He touched her arm lightly. "Get back in the chair. You're in no condition to do this alone." He realized in that moment that he was making a commitment to keep her safe until he could hand her over to the police. It was a commitment he was willing to make for Jamie's sake. Matthew's mother had been his saving grace growing up without a father. He sensed Rochelle possessed the same maternal strength. Without at least one parent, Jamie didn't have any kind of a shot. Matthew couldn't let that happen to a child when he had the power to prevent it.

Her shoulders drooped, and she turned back toward him, nearly falling into his arms. He lowered her into the chair. At the door, he peered up and down the hall. When he saw Blondie lean in to check a room a few doors down, he pushed the chair into the hallway. He quickened his pace but not so much as to call attention to himself.

"It's him, isn't it?" Rochelle's voice came out in a harsh whisper as she bent her head down so her long brown hair hid her face.

Matthew spoke under his breath. "He's behind me. He can't see you, and he doesn't know who I am." Matthew slipped into a supply closet and pulled his phone off his belt. He dialed the police station. "I need to talk to a police officer."

A crisp female voice came on the line. "This is Officer Bridget O'Connor. How can I help you?"

"Listen, this is Matthew Stewart over at the hospital. I've got a woman who needs to be hospitalized, and I believe there is a physical threat against her. She was assaulted earlier today at her home and now there is a different guy searching the hospital for her."

"We can send an officer over to talk with her and take it from there," said Officer O'Connor.

"That sounds good. If he could meet us by Admitting, that would be great."

He hung up the phone.

Rochelle looked up at him in earnest. "He's going to meet us here?"

He was struck by how helpless she seemed sitting in the wheelchair. "We'll be in Admitting. There's lots of people around. I'll stay with you until we're sure you have the protection you need or that guy is taken into custody."

"But that man hasn't technically done anything to me, and he's not the real problem," she said.

"Maybe, but they can stop him and question him. And you can at least give them the description of the guy who grabbed you at your house, the one with the scar."

"What if the police say that there is no reason to provide protection?" Her voice filled with anxiety. "Taking those two men into custody won't make it stop. There is a different man behind all of this."

Again, he wondered exactly what she was up against. She looked as though she might cry. Compassion flooded through him. Lindy the nurse was wrong. He didn't have a rescue complex. Rochelle needed his help. He couldn't abandon her and that kid now. "We'll cross that bridge when we get to it. Let's see what the police say. I'll stay with you until we get this taken care of. You need to focus on your recovery."

She looked up at him for a long moment, probably trying to figure out why he was going to all this trouble. "Can I have your phone so I can call my son? I need to know that he's okay at my friend's house."

He placed the phone in her hand, opened the door to

the supply closet and backed the wheelchair out. "Everything is going to be all right. I'll see to it that you get well so you can take care of that kid of yours. It would help if you told me why these men are after you—"

Matthew heard the thud of a single footstep. The blow to the back of his head caused an explosion in his brain. The last thing he heard as his cheek collided with the floor was Rochelle's anguished scream.

THREE

"You're coming with me, lady."

The blond thug jerked her up out of the wheelchair, making her dizzy from the pain. There were no other people in the hallway. The empty nurses' station suggested the wing might be unused. Panic washed over her like a wave.

Rochelle did not have the strength to resist the man as he dragged her toward the exit. She turned to stare down at Matthew, who had already begun to stir. "Who are you?"

"Look, lady, I was hired by a man. I'm supposed to take you to him."

"The man you work for is a bad man. He wants to kill me." She tried to pull her arm free, causing her to drop Matthew's phone. The thug kicked the phone down the hall out of view. Pain sliced through her torso like a thousand tiny knifes.

"That's not true." Blondie squeezed her good arm tighter. "Just come on. He said you'd be resistant. He only wants to talk."

She doubted Elwood only wanted to chat. Why go to all this trouble for a conversation? The only thing

Corben wanted from her was her silence, and the only way he could get that would be to murder her. It seemed odd, though. If Corben wanted her dead, why not hire someone to kill her outright?

With a grip like iron on her upper arm, Blondie pushed her toward the exit. Any resistance she put up only caused more discomfort and made her light-headed. He led her out a side door into the employee parking lot, which unfortunately was empty. He shoved her into the back of the car. She laid her head against the leather seat. The pain had grown so intense she was having a hard time focusing let alone moving.

He grabbed her uninjured arm and pushed it upward toward the one in the sling. He pulled a piece of wire from his back pocket and secured her hands together with the insides of the wrists touching each other. She glanced around hoping, praying, that someone had seen them. He placed a blindfold over her eyes and then pushed on her shoulder. "Now get down."

The thug got into the front seat and sped off through the parking lot. Any hope that Matthew would recover fast enough to help her faded. He'd already done more than any stranger should have and for that she was grateful. But now she was on her own.

Her captor swerved through traffic and then picked up speed. They must be headed out of town. She tried to push herself up, but when the pain intensified, she collapsed onto the seat. Her heart raced as fear surrounded her every thought.

This was it then. She wouldn't see Jamie again. He was all that mattered to her. Jamie had guardians, a nice couple from her church. She'd made the legal arrangements shortly after he was born. He'd be loved and taken care of, but she wouldn't be with him. Images of her son as a baby and a toddler flashed through her mind. Her eyes warmed with tears. He was her whole life.

She slipped in and out of consciousness, uncertain how much time had passed. At one point, the noise the tires made indicated that the road had changed from paved to dirt. The car came to a stop, and she heard the driver's-side door open. She struggled to push herself up, but putting any kind of pressure on her injured arm was excruciating.

The back door opened. She assumed it was the thug until she heard a soft tenor voice. "Rochelle, it's me." Matthew slipped the blindfold off her.

She stared into the deep brown of his eyes, and gratitude washed over her.

He tugged on the sleeve of her good arm. "He's making a phone call. Sounds like he's lost and getting directions. Crawl out this way so he doesn't see you."

She inched across the seat, careful to keep her head down. Matthew's courage amazed her. If it wasn't for him, Elwood might have a gun to her head right now. She slipped out of the car and crouched, taking in her surroundings. The sky had turned dark gray with the promise of evening less than half an hour away. They were on a country road. Elwood must have rented a secluded cabin somewhere. The thug continued to talk on the phone and look out at his surroundings, probably trying to assess where he was.

Matthew pulled her into the cover of the trees and then quickly untwisted the wire that bound her hands together. "My car is down the road. I turned around when I saw he'd stopped."

Twenty feet away, she could hear the shouts and ex-
pletives of the blond thug as he realized she'd escaped.

Matthew grabbed her good hand. "Come on, it's not
far." He pulled her through the shelter of the trees. Out
of breath and barely able to walk, she stopped and bent
over. He wrapped his arm around her waist and all but
carried her the remaining distance. Finally Matthew's
car came into view. She yanked open the passenger-side
door, glancing over her shoulder. Blondie's car rounded
the corner. Matthew pressed the accelerator of his car
just as she sat in the seat and closed the door. She belted
herself in. Every part of her body felt like it was on fire
and each inhale caused physical anguish.

She glanced over at Matthew, who focused on the
road in front of him. What was going on with him that
he would take this kind of risk for her?

Matthew gained speed. The other car loomed dangerously close.

He gripped the wheel tighter and pressed the accelerator to the floor.

The other car bumped against them. Rochelle braced
herself on the dashboard with her good hand as her heart
beat out a wild rhythm. There was a second and a third
bump and then their car rolled down a steep hill. The
front end impacted with a fallen log, coming to a jerky
stop. She flew forward but the seat belt held her in place.
Her whole torso flared from the trauma.

Matthew's hand touched her shoulder. Concern filled
his voice. "You all right?"

The intensity of the pain nearly blinded her, but she
managed a nod. The warmth of his touch calmed her.

His hand brushed over her cheek. "I'm so sorry. The
last thing you needed was to be in another accident." He

stared at her so intensely it was clear he was doing his paramedic thing and assessing her responses.

"Why are you doing all of this?"

He looked directly at her. "I just figure a kid who doesn't have a dad deserves to at least have his mom around."

His comment pierced straight through her. He was willing to do all of this for Jamie.

He clicked the key in the car, but nothing happened. "I've talked to your kid a couple of times when we ran into each other in the neighborhood. He's a good kid. He deserves a shot at a normal life." He shook his head. "I don't think this car is going to start."

Still reeling from what he had said about Jamie, Rochelle was seeing Matthew in a new light. For nine years, she'd been alone in caring about Jamie's future. With Dylan gone, she'd assumed it would always be that way.

Rochelle glanced around. They'd rolled down a steep, snowy embankment. The road was above them, a forest on the other side. Blondie had hit them with such force that his own car had rolled down the hill, too. It was upright, but the smashed roof indicated that it must have turned over at least once.

Matthew tried his car one more time. Clearly it wasn't going to start. He drew his attention to the thug's wrecked car. "I'm going to make sure that guy is okay. And see if his car will run."

Rochelle was amazed. Matthew never stopped being a paramedic. Blondie had nearly killed them, and Matthew still cared enough about his fellow human being to check on him.

"Be careful," she said.

"I can handle it. He's not getting out of the vehicle. He's probably incapacitated." Matthew pushed open the door and stepped out.

She waited for a moment and then thought it would be better if Matthew didn't confront their pursuer alone. Still in pain, Rochelle pushed herself from the car and trailed behind Matthew. She watched him reach through the broken window of the thug's car and touch the unconscious man's neck to make sure he had a pulse.

Concern filled his expression when he noticed her. "You should've stayed in the car."

"I was worried the guy might hurt you," she said.

"I'm not sure how much help you would have been. You're in pretty rough shape." The corner of his mouth turned up and a smile danced in his eyes. "We need to call for help." He looked down at his belt. "I don't suppose you have my phone?"

"I dropped it when he grabbed me." She peered inside the car. "His phone must be in there somewhere." She went around to the passenger-side door and opened it to search.

Blondie's eyes shot open. He grabbed her hair and started pulling. "You." His voice filled with rage. Her scalp burned.

Matthew ran up behind her, wrapped his arm around her waist and wrestled her free. The thug crawled across the seat, reaching out for her, but Matthew pulled her back. The thug emerged from the wrecked car, swaying on his feet. His injuries from the accident had left him debilitated, and he stalked toward them slowly, stopping frequently. Matthew helped Rochelle sit down. After patting the thug down for a weapon, he led him back to the car where he tied him up. Weakened by the accident and his outburst with Rochelle, the thug resisted only once.

After returning to Rochelle, Matthew glanced up at the road above them and then at the forest. "Follow me." He raced over to his wrecked car and pulled a first-aid kit out of the backseat.

She staggered toward him. Her side hurt every time she wheezed in air.

He must have seen the pain in her expression. "You can't keep running like this. It will mess you up more. You can't walk back to town in your condition." He stared up at the steep incline that led to the country road.

"We have to at least try," she said. "Someone should be along to pick us up."

She swayed, and he wrapped an arm around her waist. He glanced over his shoulder to where the thug remained slumped against the car. "Guess we don't have a lot of options. We'll call for someone to come and get him when we get to town. I've got you. Walk as fast as you can."

They made it only a short way up the hill before she stopped, breathing heavily and leaning against him. This wasn't going to work. She could hardly walk, let alone climb a hill.

"I don't think we should stay out in the open long. Other people might be coming when that guy doesn't show up with me," she said.

He walked parallel to the road, still supporting Rochelle. "Where was that guy taking you?"

"He was taking me to a man, an evil man who I am pretty sure wants me dead."

"Why does he want you dead?" He continued to hold her up and plodded forward.

"Because…I…witnessed him…kill a man. Jamie's father." Recalling the horror of ten years ago weakened her even more. Her knees buckled.

He caught her in his arms and then looked directly at her. His hand touched her cheek. "You need to get your strength back up. You can't walk anymore."

"Maybe it's not such a good idea to go up there anyway." She was having a hard time forming a complete thought. "They'll be looking for us on that road when I don't show up."

"We'll have to come up with a different plan, then," said Matthew. He pulled her into the shelter of some trees. He ripped open the first-aid kit and doled out two pills from a packet. "Take these. They'll help somewhat with the pain." His face was etched with concern. "What you need more than anything is rest. We'll have to walk awhile on the flat ground, find a hiding place. Can you do that for me?" He shoved other items from the kit in his pockets.

She nodded even as she felt herself growing light-headed. She peered over her shoulder wondering if the thug would be able to figure out which direction they'd gone and tell whoever showed up. The snow was patchy and their footprints faint. "I guess hiding is our best option for now."

With Matthew supporting her, they walked until they came to a place where the tree cover was fairly thick. He gathered tree branches and laid them on top of the snow. Using the branches as a chair, Matthew helped Rochelle to the ground.

"You need to stay here and rest. I'm going to scout

around and see if there is another more accessible road where we might be able to catch a ride into town."

"What if they come looking for me or that man in the car gets away?"

Matthew knelt beside her. He touched her cheek with his palm. The warmth of his touch seeped through her skin. "I know this plan is not perfect, but I will do everything in my power to make sure you get back to the hospital and get well for your son."

"This is above and beyond your job description."

He hesitated. "It's what I need to do." He dug through his pockets and pulled out a granola bar. "In case you get hungry." He removed his winter coat and placed it around her shoulders.

"I won't be gone for more than forty-five minutes. If anyone does come looking for you, you should be able to hear him coming. Find a place to hide. I'll come back for you. I promise."

How long would it be before Elwood realized something had happened and he came looking for her? "Won't you be cold?" The sweater Matthew wore looked like it was wool, but it couldn't totally shut out the November chill.

"You're the one who needs to stay warm. Rest. Try to regain your strength. I'll find a way to get you back to the hospital so you can get better."

"Thank you." Though she doubted she'd be safe in that hospital, she was overwhelmed by the extent to which he had gone to help her.

Matthew tilted his head. "It's almost dark. That works in our favor." He turned on a flashlight that was attached to his key chain and set off, his footsteps crunching in the snow. The noise slowly faded. Rochelle sat in the dark listening for the sound of approaching footsteps.

Matthew wasn't wrong. Both accidents had weakened her. She was in no condition to travel, but what choice did she have? She slipped into Matthew's coat, surprised by how warm it was. The coat smelled like him, kind of a woodsy musk scent. Her heart was opening up to him in a way that hadn't happened since Dylan's death. Yet she didn't trust her own feelings. These were desperate circumstances, and Matthew had made it clear that his concern was only for her physical health and a secure future for Jamie. She didn't dare read more into his kindness than that.

Despite her hypervigilance, exhaustion overtook her and she nodded off, grateful for the warmth of Matthew's coat and for his help. She only hoped he was able to find a way back into town before Elwood Corben's brand of trouble caught up with her again.

Matthew crossed his arms over his chest to stave off the evening cold. He'd be all right as long as he kept moving. His back muscles ached more than they should have. He'd probably strained them in the accident. He might be sore tomorrow, but he didn't think he'd sustained much damage.

So far he hadn't seen anything resembling a road. He hated leaving Rochelle behind. But he would have done more damage making her follow him around with no clear direction to go. He'd made a tough choice when there were no good choices.

Rochelle hadn't been exaggerating when she said she needed to leave town. Clearly, her life was being threatened. Her initial solution had been to run, but she was in no condition for any kind of travel. When they got back into town, he'd have to convince her of that. The police had to provide some kind of protection and find the man responsible for all she had gone through.

He shone his flashlight all around, still not seeing any sign of a road or an alternate route back into town. He slowed down in his jogging.

What had he gotten himself into? Rochelle had witnessed a murder. He was in way over his head. Had he been right to trust his gut feeling or had he been impulsive in thinking he had to rescue Rochelle and her son? His sense of duty had to end somewhere. As soon as he handed her safely over to the police, he could step back from all of this.

He'd had a moment after he'd been knocked down at the hospital that he'd thought to run back to where people were and get a nurse to call the police, but he knew he had only seconds to catch up with Rochelle and her abductor before she'd be lost for sure and then Jamie would be an orphan.

He checked his watch. He could search another ten minutes and still have time to get back to Rochelle if he ran. The looming darkness made everything look different, but his experience as a hiker had forced him to pay attention to landmarks in all kinds of conditions. He'd find his way back just fine.

His boots crunched on the snow, and a chill settled over his skin. He walked faster, shining the light in an arc. The silhouette of a structure came into view. He walked toward it and realized it was a house with no lights on. Probably nobody home. All the same, he knocked. He waited, staring up at the night sky, which had grown darker. Stars twinkled down at him, and the full moon provided some illumination. He knocked again, this time louder, praying that lights would come on and someone would open the door.

He peered in the window but couldn't see much. The place might not be occupied year-round. There were plenty of vacation cabins out this way. It could be months before the owners came back. There was no garage, and he didn't see a car anywhere. As expected, when he tried the door it was locked.

He needed to get back to Rochelle. As he ran, he weighed his options. Rochelle would be feeling a little stronger after resting. They might be able to hike out to the country road where the accident had occurred. They'd have the cover of darkness in their favor, and they could walk parallel to the road until they found a place that was less steep. He stuttered in his step. Not the best plan. He had no idea what additional injury Rochelle had suffered from the second accident and he wasn't doing too great, either. His best guess was that she wouldn't be able to walk very far. They would have to hope a car picked them up right away.

Rochelle had been pretty certain the thug had friends who would come looking for her. Her kidnapper had been in rough shape, but it was probably too much to hope that he would just get a ride back into town.

Matthew pushed tree branches out of the way. He was getting close to where he'd left Rochelle. He shone the light. He could see where the snow was pressed down and the pile of branches he'd gathered for her to sit on, but no Rochelle. He wasn't panicked. She might have gotten up to keep warm.

He followed the footprints in the snow that indicated which direction she'd gone, but they ended abruptly in a dry patch of ground. He was about to call her name when he heard a rustling in the trees, and then a man grunted. He turned off his flashlight and slipped behind an evergreen.

The crunching of footsteps told him the man was maybe ten feet away. Matthew scanned the darkness. Rochelle must have heard the man coming and hidden somewhere, too. He caught a flash of color as the man walked past him—not the same man who had been in the car accident, not Blondie. This guy was thin. He waited for the footsteps to fade. He could still see the flashlight bobbing in and out of the trees moving farther away.

"Rochelle." Matthew's voice came out in a harsh whisper. His muscles tensed when he didn't hear anything.

He angled out from behind the tree and returned to where he'd seen her footprints. He slipped into the forest. When he looked over his shoulder, the flashlight of the thug was coming back toward the clearing.

He darted through the trees, his feet pounding against the frozen ground. His voice filled with desperation as he whispered, "Rochelle."

"I'm here." She appeared out of the darkness, still wearing his coat.

He grabbed her hand. "He's coming back this way."

He pulled her through the forest. He could hear the rapid crunching of their footsteps. The light came directly toward them. They'd been spotted. With Rochelle lagging behind him as he held on to her hand, he knew they weren't going to outrun this guy. He guided her toward some brush hidden from the moonlight by a canopy of trees. They huddled low and close together waiting for the sound of passing footsteps. He listened to the ragged exhale and inhale of her breath. All this movement was hard on her. Moments later, footsteps crunched through the dry snow. They remained still, their shoulders touching, until the noise faded.

Finally, she released a heavy breath. "I think he's gone…for now."

"We should get up to the road." What choice did they have but to try to get out that way? He rose to his feet and put out a hand to help her up. She groaned in pain as she got to her feet. The accident and all the running had weakened him, too. If his muscles ached, hers must be in worse shape.

As though she'd heard his thoughts, she said, "I'm okay." But the waver in her voice gave away how much pain she was in.

He took her hand. "Hopefully, a driver will come along quickly before that guy comes back."

They wove through the evergreens, finally emerging from a cluster of trees. Matthew dove to the ground, taking Rochelle with him. She groaned when she hit the ground. Two cars with the lights on were parked along the road. He lifted his head and counted at least three men patrolling the road.

Rochelle gasped, her voice filled with fear. "That's Elwood Corben, the man who's after me."

She pointed toward a man standing beside one of the cars.

What could they do? Rochelle couldn't keep moving, not in her condition. Running in the valley parallel to the road until they were out of sight of the patrollers might be too much for her. This Elwood Corben had brought some manpower with him. What if he had someone patrolling the road in a car? They might have to run for miles before they were in the clear.

"Come with me. I know a place we can hide for a while." Moving away from the path, he wove through the trees, listening for the footfalls of the man searching the woods for them. Rochelle lagged behind him. When he turned to look at her, she was bent over though trudging forward. She lifted her head.

"We're almost there." He pressed his hands against her cheeks. "Can you make it?"

She nodded but then her head tilted back as she swayed. He caught her and carried her the remaining distance to the cabin, setting her on her feet outside the door. She continued to lean against him for support while he broke the window and reached in to unlatch the door. Because crime was not a huge issue around here, security measures were usually not extensive. He'd leave a note with his phone number explaining why they'd broken in and offering to pay for the window.

The cabin was one large room with an adjoining bathroom. Whoever lived here had left behind a minimum of possessions. Rochelle collapsed onto a couch that must fold out into a bed. He found a blanket and laid it over the top of her. He dare not build a fire in case the men got this far out with their search. His guess, though, was that they'd be watching the road for a long time before they changed tactics on their search.

The gash on her head had begun to bleed again. He dressed it and dug through his pockets for the remaining ibuprofen. There was no running water but he found some tomato juice in the pantry. She took the pill.

Worry colored her expression. "What are we going to do if they come here?"

"I'll stay awake. If we have to run, we'll run. As soon as we have a little light, we'll find a way back into town."

"I know you want me back in the hospital." She gazed up at him with wide brown eyes. "But when we get back to town, we have to get my son first. Please."

"Of course." After all this, her focus was still her son. He slid down to the floor using the couch as a backrest. He wondered what he had gotten himself into. In a million years, he couldn't imagine that all of this was because of a murder. "Rochelle, why didn't you go to the police when you witnessed this man kill Jamie's father?"

She closed her eyes and covered them with her hand. "He threatened to hurt my family. It was ten years ago. I was young and scared and I ran away. But now he's found me."

"You can go to the police now and tell them everything that happened then and today. They will help you." She looked so forlorn, so defeated, that he didn't regret listening to his gut feeling. Rochelle had needed him. Still, he was in over his head.

There was a long moment of silence before she answered. "I want to believe that, but I saw Corben talking to a cop in the courthouse and…this is a small police department and he's a powerful man. He's had police on his payroll in Seattle."

Her voice faded.

He rose to his feet, needing to get an idea of the layout of the house and to think over what she had said. She grabbed his hand.

"Matthew, you didn't have to do all this, but I probably wouldn't be alive without you."

Her hand felt like silk in his. As he looked into her eyes, affection for her tugged at his heart. He pushed his feelings aside. The trouble she faced was complicated. Way more than he had bargained for. Whatever had sparked inside him in that moment when she touched his hand—this was not the time or place to dwell on it.

"Yeah, well, it was for the kid." He pulled away and wandered through the house, not finding anything useful—some canned goods, but not a gun or anything he could use in self-defense. When he returned to the sofa, she was fast asleep.

He listened until her breathing became steady and deep. She looked almost peaceful as she slept. He found another blanket that he wrapped around his shoulders. He slipped down to the floor using the couch as a backrest. His reaction to her thank-you surprised him. Maybe it was just about all they had been through in the past ten hours. Women he'd rescued on calls sometimes sought him out afterward. He recognized that glow of affection when they said thank-you, and he knew that relationships born out of trauma never worked out.

The best thing to do was to get Rochelle back to town and call the police so that kid had a fighting chance at a normal life.

Ten minutes passed and he felt himself nod off and jerk awake, bracing for the possibility that Elwood Corben and his thugs might burst through the door at any moment.

FOUR

Rochelle awoke to the soft touch of Matthew's hand on her shoulder. "We have to go." His voice held a note of panic that tore her away from the incoherency of sleep.

Her eyes shot open and she sat up. Her rib cage still ached but the rest had helped. "They're here, aren't they?"

In the dark cabin, shadows covered Matthew's face. "I saw lights coming through the trees. If we hurry, we can slip out before they get here."

He took her hand and guided her toward the door, easing it open. They slipped out into the dark night. Like beacons, the flashlights of their pursuers appeared and disappeared. She counted three bobbing lights in all, three men moving toward them at a rapid pace. Though she felt stronger, they still faced the same dilemma. How were they going to get back into town?

Matthew guided her through the evergreens in the general direction of the country road. He must have some kind of plan. As they slipped into the cover of the trees, voices and the breaking of branches pressed on her ears. Though they were maybe twenty yards apart, they moved in the opposite direction of their pursuers.

She pushed past her fear.

"Go, now," Matthew whispered in her ear.

She ran flat out, keeping up with Matthew. After ten minutes, her side began to hurt. She slowed down, as did Matthew beside her.

His voice filled with concern. "You doing all right?"

She nodded, trying to catch her breath. "How are we going to get away?"

"More of them must have come. That means there are cars parked along the road. We have to hurry. Can you keep going?"

Again, she nodded even though taking a deep breath caused pain to slice through her rib cage. The cabin had been at least a twenty-minute run from the road. She wasn't sure if she would make it.

"If we can find a place where the hill isn't too steep… I think I have a plan." He stood close enough to her that she could see the intensity in his gaze. He nodded as a way of encouraging her. "Let's go."

She found strength in his words and fell in step behind him. They moved through the darkness. Her ears tuned into the sounds around her. If the men who were headed toward the cabin had already doubled back, they were too far away for her to hear them. By the time they emerged through the trees, she could discern the nuances of shadows that indicated where the road was, but she didn't see any cars.

They slowed their pace, and he walked beside her. The road wasn't as steep as where the accident had occurred. He helped her up the incline.

"Here, move off to the side, where we can't be spotted." He tugged her sleeve.

"How far away do you think we are from the cars?"

"I'm not sure," he said.

Their feet crunched in the snow as they took cautious but quick steps through the darkness. With each turn in the road, she hoped the outline of cars would come into view. The pain was not as bad as it had been before but she tired easily. She couldn't walk much farther.

The dome light inside a car was the first thing she saw. A man sat behind the wheel and a second one paced around the car. When they were within a hundred yards of the parked car, Matthew slipped into a crouch, and she followed, pressing close to him.

He turned toward her and whispered, "There's another car behind that one."

She squinted, trying to see what he saw.

"If we can get to it without being noticed, that's our ride. Stay low and close to me." He inched forward. They were on the opposite side of the road from where the car with the man inside was parked. The pacing man leaned against the back of the car to have a cigarette. The darkness and the slope of the road provided some minimal cover as they eased past the car with the light on. Up ahead, she saw the car Matthew had been able to make out. It was parked at an angle on the shoulder of the road.

As they passed the occupied car, her breath caught. The man in the car was Elwood Corben.

Matthew tugged on her sleeve. They went around the far side of the unoccupied car. Matthew indicated that she should crawl in first. She did so, keeping her head down below the dashboard. Matthew crawled in and pulled some wires out from beneath the dashboard. He pressed two wires together and the car started.

So Matthew could hot-wire a car. "Where did you learn to do that?"

Matthew grinned. "Misspent youth." He shifted into gear. "Here goes nothing."

As the car lurched forward, Rochelle lifted her head up slightly. Corben had gotten out of the car and was glaring at them. His henchman stood beside him and lifted a gun to take aim on Rochelle. Terror immobilized her.

"Get back down." Matthew's voice seemed to come from far away.

Rochelle fixated on the gun. Corben placed his hand on the shooter's arm so the gun pointed at the ground instead of at her. Rochelle shook her head in disbelief. Matthew's hand covered her shoulder, and she slipped down out of view.

That didn't make any sense. Corben was hunting her like wild game and yet he had forgone the opportunity to kill her outright? Why?

Matthew sped down the dark gravel road. "Soon as they get their car turned around they'll be after us."

He increased his speed. Rochelle glanced over her shoulder, where menacing headlights glowed.

Matthew maneuvered the car with skill, and when they met up with a paved road he drove even faster. Rochelle gripped the door handle, and her heartbeat drummed in her ears. She really didn't need to be in a third car wreck today.

"Sorry, we gotta go fast if we want to lose these guys," said Matthew.

He continued to put distance between himself and the pursuers. When the headlights of the other car were no longer in sight, he slowed the car and took an un-expected turn.

"I know a back way into town," he said. "They won't be able to follow us now."

Rochelle loosened her grip on the armrest a little. She was exhausted and all the old pain had returned tenfold. She hoped Matthew was right about escaping Elwood's grasp...at least for now.

Matthew slowed the car and breathed a sigh of relief as the lights of Discovery came into view. The adren-aline surge from running still kept him vigilant. He glanced over at Rochelle, who had nodded off several times. Though she had not complained, he knew she really couldn't take much more physically.

Her eyes shot open. She glanced over her shoulder and then up ahead. "I have to go get Jamie."

"Rochelle, you need to be in a hospital. You've got to drop this idea of traveling anywhere right now." He wanted to ease her concern. "We'll give your friend a call to make sure he's doing okay. How does that sound?"

She was quiet for a long moment. "I would just feel better if I could be with my son."

"Is your son in some kind of danger from this El-wood Corben?"

She shook her head. "Elwood doesn't know Jamie exists." She glanced out the window and then down at her hands. "Maybe you're right. If I could just talk to Jamie on the phone... I know he's safe with my friend."

She winced. Maybe the pain she was feeling had won the argument for him.

"We'll call the police as soon as we get to the hospital," he said. "Then you'll be safe there."

A worried look flashed across her face. "I'm not sure if a small-town police force would be much of a match for Elwood Corben."

"We have to at least try." The look on her face was pensive, and he wondered if she was still trying to figure out a way to leave Discovery.

When they came to the edge of town, he hit the blinker and turned onto the street that led to the hospital. At this hour, there were hardly any cars in the lot.

He found a parking space that was close. When he ran around to Rochelle's side of the car, she had opened the door but was struggling to get out. He wrapped his arm around her waist and lifted her up. She leaned most of her weight on him, her breathing labored.

He looked toward the lit entrance of the hospital. A man stood outside, glancing one way and then the other while he paced. The hairs on the back of Matthew's neck stood up. At this distance, he couldn't tell if it was one of the thugs they'd encountered earlier. He had the same muscular build, but the man could just be waiting for someone.

"I see him. Is there another entrance?" Rochelle's voice was icy.

She was thinking the same thing. Why take the chance?

"Yeah, we can go around to the back." They returned to the car. He lowered her into the seat. Her raspy breathing indicated that she wasn't doing so well.

He shifted the car into gear and swung around to the back entrance of the hospital. A second man paced in front of that entrance. This one had a similar build to the man with the scar who had confronted Rochelle by her house.

Rochelle slipped down into the seat. "What now?"

Matthew turned the car around and headed back toward the street. His mind raced, struggling for a solution. "We can go to my sister's house. She's a naturopathic doctor. She lives outside of town."

"What about Jamie?"

"We'll swing around and pick him up." When he checked the rearview mirror, the man was no longer standing by the entrance, but a car had slipped in behind them. Again, this could be nothing, but the thugs at the hospital had probably been informed of the make and model of the car they'd taken for their escape.

Snow sprinkled from the sky as he pulled out onto the street. Traffic was light at this hour. It was easy enough to track that the car stayed with them.

"Do you want to know the address where Jamie is?"

"I think we'd better wait on that." He nodded toward the back of the car.

She craned her neck. "I know you're right. We can't risk leading them to Jamie." Her voice was filled with anguish.

He knew it was torture for her to be away from her son this long. "We'll figure out a way to ditch these guys and then get to my sister's." Matthew turned into Lewis and Clark Park. "We'll call and have your friend bring Jamie to us in the morning. That way, he'll be safe. They'll never know about him and you two will be together."

The car tailing them followed them into the park. He killed the lights and pulled into a parking space. When the car rolled past them and into the cemetery, he pulled out of the space, not turning on the lights until he got to the street.

He checked the rearview mirror twice. Both times no headlights loomed behind him. He increased speed and headed back toward the highway.

"How far out of town does she live?"

"About five miles," he said. "My sister will be able to take care of you. Once your son is safe with you, I'm going into town to talk to the police. I doubt Elwood and his buddies have figured out who I am yet."

Scarface and Blondie knew what he looked like. They might make the connection that he was a paramedic and maybe find out his name. If they did, the trail could lead to his sister's house. But he couldn't think of any other viable options. Rochelle needed medical care and rest.

He continued to watch the road behind him as the snowfall increased. He turned down several country roads before the outdoor lights of his sister's house shone in the distance.

Rochelle was sound asleep with her face pressed against the window when he rolled into the driveway. The lights inside the house came on and the sound of a barking dog greeted him.

He was tired and hungry. The sight of his older sister opening the door, cocking her head to one side and crossing her arms was a welcome one.

"Hey, sis, I could use your help." He turned slightly back toward the car. "It's a long story, but I got a woman who needs a place to rest and get strong."

A wry smile crossed Laura's face. "Found another stray, huh, little brother? Bring her in and then you can spend some time telling me the long story."

The snow continued to fall as he turned back toward the car. When he opened the passenger-side door, Rochelle's eyes fluttered open. "We're here."

She was in pretty rough shape. All the color had drained from her face. She leaned forward to get out of the car and he circled his arm around her waist.

Laura disappeared and returned a moment later with her boots on. She ran out to help him. "What has happened here?"

"She's been in two car accidents. Fractured arm, bruised ribs, possible head injury. I don't know what kind of damage was done the second time." He lifted Rochelle up and carried her.

They stepped inside. "Help her lie down on the couch," Laura said as she left the living room in a hurry.

Rochelle squeezed his shoulder as he lowered her to the couch. "I feel like I've been beaten up with sticks."

He grabbed a pillow from a nearby chair and placed it under her head. "Try resting on your side."

"Thank you." Rochelle offered him a faint smile despite the pain.

Laura returned with a steaming mug, which she set on the table by the couch. "I've got tea for you to drink. It'll help with the pain so you can sleep. First I need to assess what kind of damage we're looking at here." Laura knelt by the couch. "If you don't mind, little brother, I need to do an exam."

He knew Rochelle was in good hands, but he still hated leaving her. They'd been through a lot together in less than a day, and he felt a growing attachment to her. "I'll wait in the den." The look of earnest affection he saw in her expression didn't scare him so much this time.

He walked down a hallway and opened up a pocket door. He stepped inside a room that functioned as a television room, an office and storage facility. The dog he had heard barking earlier, a Lab named Misfit, rose from his bed in the corner, lumbered over to him and licked his hand. Misfit had only three legs.

Over the past few hours something had shifted for him. Rochelle's story had overwhelmed him at first, and he'd been ready to turn her over to the police, but now he felt a resolve to stay with her until she was safe from Elwood Corben.

He wandered around the office with his hands in his pockets. Photographs of Laura with friends and family cluttered the walls. Laura's husband had died in a climbing accident three years ago, and her only child was in college in Wyoming.

After the dog settled down, Matthew collapsed into a chair. As soon as he sat down, he realized how exhausted he was. He had meant to call the police right away to see what kind of help they could offer. But his mind wandered back on the past day. Less than twenty-four hours ago, he'd pulled his pretty neighbor out of a wrecked car. And now his life had been turned upside down. His gut feeling had not been wrong. Rochelle was in trouble and needed help. He'd been put in her life at that moment for a reason.

Did he regret listening to that inner voice? No, not at all. Despite the trouble it created for him, it was clear that Rochelle needed him. After he was rested, he'd call the police and make sure she was in safe hands. Knowing that he might not be a part of her life after that actually made him kind of sad.

She was so determined to leave town, he could not

foresee if they would even be neighbors after all of this. Maybe if they could get this guy Elwood Corben behind bars, she'd change her mind. That was a big maybe.

He could feel the heaviness of sleep setting in as his eyelids grew leaden. His muscles felt strained from the car accident on the country road. He would call the police soon enough. They were safe…for now.

Though she was not in intense pain, except for her arm, Rochelle felt a general sharp achiness. The tea had done her some good.

Laura studied her face for a long moment. "Matthew didn't say what your name was."

"Rochelle."

"Rochelle, if you don't mind lifting your shirt, I'd like to palpate your abdomen. This won't be as good as some of the fancy equipment at the hospital but I'll at least have an idea of what was injured." She touched Rochelle's stomach. "You let me know if anything hurts."

Laura finished the exam and then asked Rochelle to sit up.

Laura looked into Rochelle's eyes, narrowing her own. "So two car accidents, huh?"

"Matthew was the paramedic who got called to the first accident." Rochelle touched the bandage Matthew had placed on her forehead, remembering how gentle his touch had been.

"Did you hit your head in the second accident?"

"I don't remember." Rochelle thought for a moment. The memory was a blur. "It happened so fast."

Laura shook her head. "My brother does know how to show a girl a good time."

"Actually, I might not be alive if it wasn't for your

brother." She found herself wanting to know more about Matthew. Laura looked to be at least in her forties and Matthew couldn't be more than thirty. "He's quite a bit younger than you."

"He was the surprise baby. Quite a handful for our mom when he was a teenager."

She was having a hard time picturing Matthew giving anyone difficulty. "Well, something must have changed. He's become a caring and courageous man."

"Can't argue with you there." Laura continued her exam, pressing at Rochelle's neck and then turning her head from side to side. "Any dizziness?"

"Some. More like light-headedness," Rochelle said.

"There's some minor whiplash and maybe a concussion. More than anything, you need to be still and rest, give yourself time to heal up." Laura rose to her feet and cupped a hand on Rochelle's shoulder. "Drink the rest of the tea. Try to get some sleep."

Her thoughts returned to Jamie. "What time is it?"

"It's five in the morning."

"Can you wake me in a couple hours? I have a son. He's with a friend of mine. If it's not too much trouble, my friend can bring him here as soon as we have some daylight."

Laura studied her for a moment. A warmth came into her eyes, and her voice filled with compassion. "That won't be a problem, but you will have to tell me the whole story of how the two of you ended up at my door."

"Deal," Rochelle said.

Laura stood on the threshold that led to the kitchen. She shoved her hands into the pockets of her bathrobe. "I saw the way you looked at Matthew. He's got an overdeveloped need to rescue people, which makes him a good paramedic, but don't read anything more into that." With that, she left the room.

Rochelle could feel the heat rising up in her cheeks. She had to admit that she felt a connection with Matthew. But she had no idea the attraction would be obvious to someone she'd just met.

Rochelle detected the tone of warning in Laura's voice. She'd only been half-asleep when they'd pulled up. She'd heard what Laura said about Matthew bringing home strays. Was that how Matthew saw her? If so, she didn't need his pity.

Something went cold inside her, and she regretted opening up to him when they were at the cabin. He had pulled away since then. For nine years, it had been just her and Jamie and that was probably the way it should stay.

She sipped the tea and settled down to rest for a few hours, struggling to find a position in which she didn't feel pain. Her sleep was fitful, and she found herself waking up and watching the clock. Louise would be up and about by seven and that would give her plenty of time before Jamie headed off to school.

When she closed her eyes, she could see Jamie. He had the same dark hair and intense brown eyes as his father. He'd worn glasses since he was five. A memory of Jamie's laughter floating in from the backyard while she did dishes played at the corners of her mind. Tears stung her eyes as her throat constricted.

Would this nightmare ever be over? Elwood Corben was just too powerful. She saw no other solution but to run. The longer they stayed here, the greater the risk that he would find out about Jamie. She'd feel better when she could see her boy, wrap her arms around him and hold him.

Matthew was right about her not being strong enough to travel. But maybe if they had a few days here, she and Jamie could get on a plane. The thought of disconnecting from the life she had built here was heartbreaking. She didn't like the idea of not seeing Matthew again, either. But Jamie was her priority. To keep him safe, she had to leave town.

FIVE

Matthew watched as Rochelle paced in front of the living-room window. She'd made the call to her friend less than half an hour ago. Her obvious devotion to her son was something he admired about her. Now he regretted not getting to know her better when they were neighbors. If she went through with her plan to leave, he may have lost his chance to get to know her at all.

He picked up to the phone and dialed the police station. The admin person transferred him to an officer.

"Officer Bridget O'Connor. How may I help you?"

The same officer he had spoken to yesterday. "My name is Matthew Stewart. I'm a paramedic at the hospital. Yesterday, I phoned about a woman, Rochelle Miller—"

"I remember your call. We sent an officer over to meet you at the hospital and you never showed."

He could hear the resistance in her voice. Would she even believe what he had to say now? "I'm so sorry that you went to that trouble and we were not able to meet you there. I was not lying when I said that Rochelle is in extreme danger."

"Sir, we are sworn to protect the citizens of Discovery, but we don't appreciate wasting taxpayer dollars on crank calls." Officer O'Connor's voice remained professional but her words were clipped. He wasn't going to win any popularity contests where the Discovery PD was concerned.

"It wasn't a crank call. Men are after her. A man named Elwood Corben is trying to kill her because she witnessed him murder his son, Dylan Corben, in Seattle."

Her voice filled with skepticism. "When was this murder?"

"Ten years ago," he said.

"Hold on." He could hear the faint sound of her typing on a computer keyboard. She came back on the line a few minutes later. "Sir, don't make me file charges against you. Harassing the police is against the law."

"What are you talking about?"

"There is no record of a Dylan Corben having been murdered or even dying in Seattle in the time frame you gave me."

Matthew gripped the phone a little tighter. From the kitchen where he'd made the call, he could see Rochelle. She'd stopped pacing and was sitting on the sofa, looking at a magazine on the coffee table. Her long brown hair covered her face. He cleared his throat. "I don't understand." This didn't make any sense. What motivation did Rochelle have to lie about this?

"I need to ask that you quit calling us unless you have a real crime to report."

Matthew's mind was still running a hundred miles an hour when he apologized to Officer O'Connor and said goodbye.

He stepped into the living room. Rochelle glanced

up at him and offered him a soft smile. Her attention was drawn to movement outside before he could speak.

"They're here. Jamie is here." She flung open the door and ran outside.

Matthew came and stood at the window. He saw Rochelle gather Jamie into her arms. A moment later, she hugged the woman who had brought him. Snow continued to fall as the friend got back in her car and pulled out of the driveway.

Rochelle wrapped her arm around her son and headed back toward the house. As she stepped inside and stomped her feet to get the snow off her boots, he wondered if he'd totally misread who she was.

Had his extreme sacrifice been for a woman who had lied to him?

The look on Matthew's face was perplexing to Rochelle. He seemed almost angry at her. She touched Jamie's head. "Do you know this guy?"

Jamie stepped forward and held out his hand. "Yeah, from the neighborhood."

Matthew offered him a hardy handshake, but then his gaze darted up toward Rochelle. Was that suspicion she saw in his eyes? "Is everything okay?"

"We'll talk later." His words contained an iciness that she hadn't heard from him before.

Laura came to the doorway that connected the living room and the kitchen. "Breakfast is ready." She looked at Jamie. "You must be Jamie. I'm Laura."

"Pleased to meet you." Jamie did a three-sixty in the living room. "This is a very nice house you have here."

Rochelle beamed with pride for her son and the little man he'd become. She'd been so afraid on the day he was born. She was cut off from her family and uncertain if she had what it took to be a mom.

"Well, let's eat," Laura said.

Matthew entered the kitchen ahead of his sister. Rochelle wrapped an arm around Jamie. "You have no idea how glad I am to see you, kiddo."

"Mom, what's going on? How long are we going to stay at this place? Why did Louise pick me up from school and why did I spend the night at her house?"

Rochelle felt a stab to her heart. Jamie had no idea what had gone on before he was born. She had simply told him that his father was dead. And now his whole life was about to be uprooted. "I'm not sure what we're going to do." She squeezed his shoulder. She couldn't tell him they needed to leave town, not just yet. He'd been through enough already.

When they sat down to breakfast, Laura carried most of the conversation. Matthew's sullenness was disconcerting.

After they finished the bacon and eggs, Laura turned to her. "Rochelle, I insist that you go rest in the family room. Sleep is the fastest way to healing."

"Well, I—"

"Matthew and I will keep Jamie busy."

She looked over at her son, who took a nibble of his toast. "Are you okay with that?"

He drew his eyebrows together, and she knew that he was trying to process how strange his life had become. His gaze fell on the cut on her forehead and then to her arm. "Sure, okay, Mom." His response revealed what a compliant kid he was. She knew he was confused by the sudden upheaval.

"Jamie, have you ever fed chickens?" Laura pushed back from the table.

His face brightened. "No, I love animals, though." He looked over at his mom for the okay.

"That sounds like fun, Jamie," Rochelle said. She loved to see him smile.

"Well, come on, I'll show you the ropes." Laura grabbed a coat hung by the back door. "You can meet my pet goat, Broderick."

Jamie laughed at the name. "Okay."

"Let's see if we can find some winter gear for you. That snow is really coming down."

Laura and Jamie's voices faded as they went into the back entryway. Matthew stayed behind, his demeanor still chilly.

"What's going on?" She was almost afraid to hear the answer. "Why are you mad at me?"

"When I called the police, they said there was no record of a Dylan Corben dying or being murdered or even reported missing."

Rochelle took in a sharp breath as her thoughts raced. "That can't be. I saw him die."

Matthew tossed his napkin on the table. "Did you?" His chair screeched as he pushed it back.

Rochelle's mind reeled with what he had told her. She'd always assumed that Corben had found a way to distance himself from Dylan's murder so he wouldn't even be a suspect, but now it looked like his body hadn't even been discovered. She shook her head. "He covered it up. Somehow he covered it up."

"Is that what it is?" Matthew turned his back to her.

Obviously Matthew doubted that she was telling him the truth. That bothered her more than anything. "Matthew, I was there. I saw it. I wouldn't make something like this up."

He turned back slowly. The look on his face was pensive as he studied her. He must know she was telling the truth. Why would she lie about something this important?

"Please, believe me." Her voice was barely above a whisper.

"I want to. I really do." He paced toward the back door. "The police here in Discovery are not overly anxious to help us right now because we didn't show up when they came to the hospital and now they think I was lying about Dylan Corben's death."

She had never believed the local police would be able to help her. Standing up to Elwood Corben was a war that no one could win.

"This doesn't need to be your problem anymore." She leaned back against the counter for support. The last thing she wanted was for him to feel betrayed. "Jamie and I have to leave town. There is no other solution. As soon as I am well enough to travel, we'll be gone. You have done more than any person should have for us."

"Sure, Rochelle. If that's what you want to do," Matthew said. "I can head back into town. Laura will get you healed up. She'll take you to the airport or bus station. Whatever you decide."

A tension-filled silence fell between them. She didn't want to part on these kinds of terms. How could she convince him she was telling the truth? She took a step toward him. Her hand hovered over his shoulder. Would he pull away if she touched him? "Matthew I—"

The phone rang, cutting her off.

"It's for Laura. Just let the machine pick it up." Matthew took a step away from her, and the room seemed to grow colder.

A frantic voice came on the line. "Oh, I hope I have the right number. I saw the name of the naturopathic business outside when I dropped Jamie off."

Rochelle bolted for the phone. "Louise, what's going on?"

"Rochelle—" Her voice broke. "I'm so sorry."

"What are you talking about?"

"Some men came to the house just when I got back. They had guns, and they threatened to hurt my kids. They showed me the picture of you and Jamie in the newspaper when he won the science fair."

"I forgot all about that photograph." The newspaper article had run the day before Corben showed up. How could she have let her guard down and allowed her and Jamie to be photographed? Still gripping the phone, Rochelle closed her eyes and sank to the floor. Corben knew about Jamie. That's why he hadn't killed her. He needed her to lead him to Jamie first.

Alerted to her distress, Matthew came and stood beside Rochelle.

Louise's voice seemed to come from far away. "I told them where I'd taken Jamie. I'm so sorry. They would have hurt my kids if I didn't."

Rochelle felt like she couldn't breathe, as if a heavy weight had been laid on her chest. "They're coming out here?"

"They left maybe five minutes ago." Louise paused for a breath. "I didn't know what to do. I'm so sorry."

Rochelle felt numb all over. "Louise, you did what you had to do to keep your kids safe. You're a good friend."

"Rochelle, I feel like I don't know you. Who were those men?"

"Thank you for everything, Louise. I have to go."

The line went dead. Rochelle leaned back against a cupboard.

Matthew knelt beside her and took the phone from her hand. Concern was etched across his face. "They're coming here, aren't they?"

She nodded as terror filled her heart.

SIX

Matthew burst to his feet. "We have to get you and Jamie out of here." When Rochelle remained on the floor, he looked down at her. "We need to go."

She tilted her head, her eyes a bit unfocused. "We?"

He still didn't know what her whole story was, but there was an innocent kid involved in all of this. He took in a deep breath. "Yes, until you two can leave town, I'll see to it that guy can't get to you." He held out a hand and pulled her off the floor.

She offered him a faint smile. "Louise said they'd just left town. With the icy roads, that probably gives us a decent head start."

Matthew retrieved their coats and gear from the living room, and they headed out the back door. They found Jamie and Laura in the barn gathering eggs.

"Jamie, we need to leave." She held out a hand to her son.

"We're not finished getting eggs." Jamie's forehead wrinkled in confusion.

She ran to him and placed her hands on his shoulders. "Baby, there are men who want to hurt us. But we're going to be okay." She looked at Matthew. "Matthew is going to help us."

Matthew watched Jamie shake his head, growing more upset. Rochelle brushed her hand over the top of his head and pulled him close. Jamie pushed his glasses up on his nose. An expression of hardness and resolve took over his features.

Laura set the basket on the hay bale. "More trouble, huh?"

He turned to face his sister. "We need a hiding place where she can recover."

Laura ran her fingers through her hair. "You can take my truck. The way this snow is coming down, that little car you came in won't get far. Why don't you head up to Jeffersonville? No one will think to look for you there."

"We'll need cold-weather gear and some food." He followed behind his sister as she headed toward the house.

Rochelle held Jamie's hand. "What's Jeffersonville?"

Matthew opened the door of the truck parked by the side of the house.

"Jamie, why don't come inside and help me gather up some stuff." Laura raced into the house with Jamie following behind her.

Matthew leaned into the truck and turned the key, which was already in the ignition. The truck roared to life. He faced Rochelle. "It's an abandoned ghost town. We need to get out there fast before they come here."

"Won't it be cold?"

"It's not the Ritz-Carlton, but we'll manage." He looked in the glove compartment to see if Laura still kept a flashlight there. "The important thing is it's not a place that can be linked back to either of us." The tightness in her mouth told him she still wasn't sure if this was a good plan. "It's the best option, Rochelle. They figured out who your friend was. Who knows what else they know by now."

She brought her hands up to her face. "I thought of that. What if they'd found out who Louise was sooner?" Her eyes glazed. "He could have taken Jamie. I can't let him leave my side again."

She had become so vulnerable and fearful. His heart went out her. He had to believe that she was telling the truth about Dylan being murdered or helping her might be an exercise in futility.

Laura returned, holding several sleeping bags. "Jamie's gathering up some food. I'm going to put together some supplies to help Rochelle." She pointed a finger at Matthew. "She needs several days to rest. No more running."

Matthew nodded. "Laura, come with us. You don't want to face down these guys."

Laura waved the idea away with her hand. "I'll be fine. I'll go to the neighbors'. They won't find anyone here when they come by. If they choose to come back another time, I'll call the police. Besides, I have a shotgun and Misfit."

Matthew hugged his sister before she ran back into the house. Within a few minutes, they had loaded the crew cab with food and other supplies. Matthew hid the car they'd hot-wired in the barn so there would not be any evidence that Elwood and his men had come to the right place.

He pulled the truck out onto a country road that looked like it hadn't been plowed.

In his side-view mirror, he could see Laura backing

out of her driveway in a four-wheel-drive car and heading in the opposite direction.

Jamie hunkered down in the seat. "I liked that farm."

Matthew's heart squeezed tight over the chaos the boy's life had become. He would do everything to make sure the boy was protected, not only physically but emotionally.

The snowfall intensified and the wind kicked up a notch. Half a foot of snow had already fallen.

Rochelle stared through the windshield at the deepening snow. "Will this truck make it?"

"It'll do fine." Matthew offered her a faint smile and then drew his attention back to the road.

Rochelle's forehead glistened with perspiration. Judging from the way she gripped the armrest, she must still be in some pain.

Matthew navigated up the winding mountain road more from memory than from what he saw in front of him. Snow had drifted across the road, making it hard to guess where the ruts even were.

Soon the gray buildings of the ghost town came into view. Some were half-hidden by accumulated snow, but he knew the layout. He'd played here with friends when he was a kid.

Jamie peered through the windshield. "What is this place?" His voice held a note of amazement.

Matthew was glad to see the kid had recovered from his previous disappointment. "It used to be a mining town and then the gold dried up and all the people went away."

"Wow," said Jamie.

There was something likable about a kid with that kind of flexibility.

"We read about the gold rush in our history book."

"Jamie loves to read," said Rochelle. Her voice sounded weak. When he looked over, her face was waxen. All this exertion wasn't good for her.

Matthew parked the truck. "Rochelle, why don't you lie down in the backseat. Jamie and I can handle setting up camp. What do you say, Jamie?"

"That sounds like fun."

For once Rochelle didn't argue with him, which was an indication of what rough shape she was in. Laura had just started to get her on the mend and they had to run again.

He already knew which building was structurally sound enough to set up camp in. That residence had a fireplace in the main room and the roof didn't leak too much. They'd use that one. The bundles of wood he'd thrown into the back of the truck would at least last them through the night.

How long would they have to stay up here before Rochelle was well enough to travel? A day? Two days?

Matthew pointed toward the house he had in mind. "Let's take the stuff into there." He grabbed the sleeping bags, and Jamie picked up the box of food.

He caught the worried look on Jamie's face when he glanced at his mother.

"So this is like an adventure, huh?" Matthew tried to distract him as they walked toward the house.

Jamie trudged through the snow. "Is my mom going to be okay?"

"If she can just get rested up."

Jamie became very solemn. "She looks like she has the flu. That's never good."

The interior of the house was dark. Matthew and

Jamie worked together to build a fire and set out the sleeping bags. While Jamie arranged the cans of food, Matthew returned to the truck to get Rochelle.

When he opened the door, she was fast asleep. She had wrapped her arms around her body. Perspiration beaded her forehead.

He touched her shoulder lightly. Her eyes fluttered open. "We've made a camp for you."

"You and Jamie did?'

"Yeah, he's a pretty helpful guy," Matthew said.

He helped her out of the truck. She leaned on him heavily as they walked the short distance to the house.

Inside, Jamie sat by the glowing fire. He turned to them and smiled. "Mom, look what we put together for you."

"This looks great, honey." There was a quiver in her voice.

A sleeping bag by a fire was a far cry from a hospital bed where she could be monitored, but it would have to do. "The sleeping bags are down and we put some cushions under yours. The fire should keep us warm." After she lay down, he made a pillow with his own coat and slipped it under her head.

He stood up to get the pain pills Laura had given him. Jamie came alongside him. The boy's hand slipped into his. "Is my mom going to be all right?" This time, the question was even more insistent.

"We're going to do our best." He tried to keep his voice positive.

He gave Rochelle the pills and made sure she was comfortable. Jamie stood off to one side, his fingers laced together. The worried look on his face had intensified.

"We still got plenty of daylight out there. Why don't we let your mom rest, and you and I can go build a snow fort."

Jamie stared at the floor.

"Come on, let's go do something outside," Matthew said.

Jamie glanced down at his mother one more time and trudged toward the door. Matthew fell in behind Jamie as they stepped out into the midday sun. Though the wind had let up a bit, flakes still sprinkled from the sky.

Jamie started a snowball, but Matthew caught the boy peering off at the house several times. They worked for a good twenty minutes, attempting to make a fort.

"The snow isn't sticking together very good." Jamie kicked at one of his snowballs.

Matthew patted his shoulder. "We gave it our best shot. Why don't we go inside and get something to eat."

"That's a good idea. I'm starving."

"Me, too, kid." They hadn't eaten since breakfast. It must be past two o'clock by now.

Inside, Rochelle slept facing the fire with her back to them. Matthew threw on several more logs. In the dim firelight, he studied Rochelle for a moment. Her face still looked like wax, and her breathing was shallow. He prayed there wasn't internal damage from the second accident. If there was, all the sleep in the world wouldn't help.

Jamie sorted through the cans in the food box. "When I went on a scouting trip we had beans and wieners. We ate it cold because we couldn't get our fire started. Looks like we have to eat this cold, too. There are no pans or anything in here to cook with."

"Yeah we sort of forgot about that," Matthew said.

"Take the labels off the cans and put them close to the fire. That will heat them up."

"Anything would taste good right now," Jamie said. He held up a can of beans and another of Spam.

"Looks like a feast."

"Do you think my mom wants to eat?"

He'd do anything to take the anxiety away from Jamie. "She really needs to rest, kiddo."

Jamie pushed his glasses back on his face. "You can call me Jamie. I am nine years old, you know."

Matthew chuckled as he pulled his Swiss Army knife out and flipped up the can opener on it. Matthew peeled the metal cover off the Spam. "We might be able to heat other stuff up in this once the Spam is gone."

"That's a good idea." Jamie's tone seemed a little more cheerful. "My pocketknife has a spoon on it."

"Get it out. We got food to eat," Matthew said.

The food disappeared quickly. Once he could use the Spam can, he melted some snow and made some of the tea his sister had sent along.

He scooted over to Rochelle and touched her cheek with the back of his hand. She didn't feel feverish. That was a good sign. "Rochelle, can you wake up? I need you to drink some of this."

She raised her head slowly. Across the floor, Jamie watched closely. She swallowed the tea and then turned toward Jamie.

"Come sit by me, sweetie," Rochelle said.

Jamie sat cross-legged beside his mother while she propped her head up with her arm. She patted his knee.

"I know you're worried, but things are going to be okay."

"Are you going to get better?"

"I'll do my best," she said. The lilt in her voice suggested she was trying to sound positive.

"Then we can go back to the house?"

She took a moment to answer. "No, Jamie, we can never go back. This man… He wants to hurt both of us. We have to find a new place to live."

Rochelle did a good job of keeping her voice neutral, but Matthew knew the anguish behind that statement.

"But we're not going to let that man hurt either of you," he said.

Jamie's shoulders drooped. "Do I have to leave my friends and everything?"

"Yes, baby, I'm so sorry. We have to go somewhere this man can't find us."

She reached out and held his hand. "I'm so sorry about this."

"It's okay, Mom."

Matthew left the two of them alone for a moment. He stepped outside. If only there was some way Rochelle wouldn't have to spend the rest of her life running, so Jamie could have a normal childhood. How could they ensure that a man like Elwood Corben would go to jail and stay in jail? Maybe it was a battle they couldn't win. Right now, he wasn't even sure if Dylan Corben was dead or if Rochelle was telling him the whole story.

Matthew scanned the road and the horizon. He saw no headlights or any sign of life. He was pretty sure they were safe up here. But he still needed to keep a close watch. Rochelle and her son weren't in the clear yet.

Rochelle laid her head back down on the makeshift pillow Matthew had given her. Jamie turned away from her and swiped the tears from his eyes. Bless his heart.

He didn't want her to see him cry. He was trying so hard to be brave. It only made her love him more.

Jamie turned back around and offered her a faint smile. "Do you need to rest some more, Mom?"

"I probably should." Though the pain had subsided some, she still felt weak and achy.

Matthew returned from outside. His gaze moved from Rochelle to Jamie. "Jamie, why don't you let your mom rest up? You and I can think of something to do."

Jamie rose to his feet. "Want to play a game?"

"We don't have any."

"Maybe we can make one up." Jamie sat down on the floor. "Maybe we can do something with the words on these cans."

Even as her body fought to deal with the pain, Rochelle smiled as she listened to Jamie and Matthew interact.

After Dylan died, there had been nobody. She'd put her energy into getting training as a court reporter, finding her faith again and being Jamie's mom. There had been men who were interested in her, but they seemed to regard Jamie as an inconvenience or as competition for her attention. She had always thought that if she did meet someone, he would have to understand that she and Jamie were a package deal.

As she listened to their laughter over the made-up game, she realized Matthew seemed to have connected to Jamie in a way no other man had.

She squeezed her eyes shut and her hand curled into a fist. Though she felt a growing affection for Matthew, why would she open herself to heartache again? Losing Dylan had nearly killed her. She didn't want to go through that ever again. She and Matthew would be parting ways in a couple of days. Tears warmed her eyes as the heaviness of sleep set in. Chills invaded her body and she wrapped herself tighter in the sleeping bag.

Matthew touched her head lightly. She felt the weight of a blanket being placed over her.

"That should help with the cold." His voice seemed to come from a long ways away.

She fell into a light sleep. The pain of her injuries woke her frequently. She focused on the crackling of the fire. The hours passed, and eventually she fell into a deeper sleep. Sometime in the night, Matthew woke her to give her more pills.

For two days, she slept and woke and ate and slept some more. The pain in her arm and rib cage grew less intense. Her interaction with Jamie and Matthew consisted of short conversations and listening to the two of them work together to find wood and keep the fire going and come up with new games to play.

Late on the second night, she fell asleep to the two of them talking about what they were carving out of wood with their pocketknives. She awoke with the sun warming her face.

Jamie and Matthew sat side by side displaying matching smiles.

"Hey, sleepyhead." Matthew's warm bass voice resonated in her head.

Jamie held up what looked like an animal carved out of wood. "Look what Matthew taught me to make."

"That looks really neat, honey." She stared at the sunlight streaming through the window with the broken glass. "How long have I been asleep?"

"Like a full twelve hours." Matthew rose to his feet. "I'm sure it was good for you."

She sat up and stretched. There was still some pain, but it was much more manageable.

"Do you feel better?" Concern was etched across Matthew's face.

She took a deep breath, and for the first time it didn't hurt. "I think I'm finally on the mend."

"Well, then," said Matthew, "I guess we can get you back into town and on an airplane."

Even though he looked down and away from her, she picked up on the disappointment in his voice.

SEVEN

From the moment they pulled into the airport parking lot, Matthew felt jittery. Maybe it was because he knew this was goodbye. He'd never see Rochelle or her charming son again. More than anything, he didn't like having to sever the bond that he and Jamie had formed. "Do you have a way to pay for a plane ticket?"

She nodded. "I have some money."

"I'll walk with you into the airport." Honestly, he wouldn't feel comfortable until she and Jamie were safe on a plane. He quelled his fear by realizing that even if Corben's men were watching the airport, they couldn't be here 24/7 and still be looking for Rochelle in Discovery. So far they had encountered Corben and at least five or six other men. That wasn't a huge amount of manpower.

They got out of the truck and walked through the ground transportation pickup area into the airport. Rochelle stared up at the departure boards.

"I guess we should try to get the first flight out of here. Jamie, you stay with Matthew until I can get our tickets."

A heaviness weighed on Matthew's shoulders as

he watched Rochelle make her way up to the counter. Three people stood in front of her in the line.

Jamie leaned against him. "I don't want to go."

He didn't want Jamie to leave, either. "You got to trust your mom, kid. She only wants the best for you."

Jamie tilted his head. His wide brown eyes rested on Matthew. "I'm going to miss you. You're fun."

He ruffled Jamie's hair. His throat went tight with emotion. This was the way things had to be.

A few feet away Rochelle stepped up to the counter and spoke to the woman for a minute. She turned back around and shook her head before checking the departure boards again and choosing a different counter.

"Can I go get a drink of water?" Jamie pointed at a water fountain some twenty feet away.

Matthew studied the people milling around the airport. None of them looked like Corben or the thugs they'd encountered. "Yeah, that would be okay. Come right back."

Rochelle returned from the second counter holding two tickets. "I guess this is it."

He stepped closer to her. "I wish you and Jamie all the best. He's a really neat kid." He hadn't intended to sound so formal, as if he was saying goodbye to a business colleague. But he didn't want to open the door to the strong emotion he'd managed to keep tamped down.

She glanced over at Jamie, who had finished getting a drink and was staring at something inside the gift store. Then she turned back toward him. "Matthew, there are no words to say thank you for all that you've done for us."

"I hope you're able to build a life somewhere...you and Jamie."

She leaned toward him and kissed him on the cheek. The honey scent of her skin lingered even as she pulled back.

"Jamie, come on, we gotta go." Jamie bolted toward his mom as she held out her hand.

He watched them go…mother and son. Jamie turned suddenly, ran back toward him and wrapped his arms around Matthew's waist.

As quickly as he'd given the hug, Jamie was back beside his mother. Rochelle mouthed the words *thank you* before they both turned and headed toward the stairs that led to the security line and the airport gates.

Matthew stepped around a corner, leaned against a pillar for support and took in a deep breath. He'd kept his word. He'd seen to it that Rochelle got healed up enough to travel. He'd made sure Rochelle and Jamie would be safe building a new life somewhere else. He was happy for them, glad they were safe again, but still he couldn't shake the empty feeling inside. They'd only known each other for a few days. Maybe it was the intensity of what they'd been through together that made him feel such loss.

And maybe his need to play rescuer had just caused him pain again. Whether it was a wild bird or a woman, his reward for doing the right thing was watching them leave.

Now all he had to do was go back to his old life, back to work. Simple enough, right? But he knew that every time he walked past Rochelle's old house, he'd think about her and her son.

He turned the corner of the terminal and spotted a pay phone in an alcove. Kind of an odd sight these days. But he was grateful for it. He doubted he would get his old cell phone back and he needed to call Laura and make sure she was okay. He needed to call work, as well. He'd missed two shifts without explanation. He dialed Laura's number and waited while it rang.

He saw movement out of the corner of his eye and then a gruff voice pounded his eardrum. "I think you better come with me."

The man pressed a hard object against the middle of Matthew's back. "What do you want?" Matthew caught a look at the man in his peripheral vision—Blondie, the muscle-bound thug who had kidnapped Rochelle.

"Just tell us where the woman and the kid are." The man poked the gun harder into Matthew's skin. "And don't get any ideas. This gun has a silencer on it. As busy as this airport is, I could drop you so fast and walk away before anyone noticed."

The man was right about that. "I don't know where the woman and her kid are going."

"Come on, Matthew. We know you were helping her."

So they had found out who he was. It wouldn't do any good to pretend he didn't know what they were talking about.

"We're going to find her one way or another," said the thug. "Now you can tell us and save us a little bit of time and we'll spare you. Or you can play the hero and end up dead."

"Jamie, come on. We've got to get in line." They had an hour and half before their flight to Indianapolis took off, but she would feel better once they got through security and were waiting at the gate.

Jamie dawdled by a display of made-in-Montana

gifts. He was dragging his feet. Rochelle knew he didn't want to get on that plane. This was the only home he'd ever known. His attachment to Matthew had grown quite strong, as well.

Jamie pressed his face against the display glass. "I don't even know where Indiana is."

"We can look it up on a map. The airplanes usually have a magazine with a map."

"What about my friend Jace? Can I call him and let him know where I am?"

Rochelle shook her head as a wave of sorrow hit her. Jamie had so much confusion to sort through.

Jamie hung his head. "We were going to build robots today."

She held out her hand. "Come on, little man. I know this isn't easy, but we have to do this."

His cool, soft hand slipped into hers. She headed toward security but stopped. She pulled Jamie back toward a pillar.

"Mom, what are you doing?"

"Shh." Her heart raced. One of the men in the security line looked like the man who had assaulted her at her house. She glanced around. Was he the only guy staking out the airport? If she could hide until the last minute and then go through security, they'd probably be okay.

"Mom, what's going on?"

She checked her watch. "I think we're going to wait awhile before we go through that line."

Jamie furled his brow. "But you said we needed to hurry." His expression changed as he watched her. He must have seen the fear in her face. "Mom?"

She stepped to the edge of the balcony and stared

down at the ground floor. The thug would be on the other side of security in a few minutes. It must be his job to look for her at the gates. Had Elwood sent others, too? She scanned the crowd. She had only a vague memory of the other men. Two of them had been broad-shouldered football-player types. One had been on the thin side.

She put an arm around Jamie's shoulder and pulled him close.

"Mom, what is it?" His voice was a fear-filled whisper.

"Oh, no." She took a step back. Down below, Matthew walked by with a blond, thick-necked man pressed close to him. The man who'd taken her from the hospital. "Jamie, we've got to get away from here." She left out the part about seeing Matthew. She didn't want to scare her son any more than she had to. Her voice was already shaky from the terror she was trying to hide.

"What about the plane?"

"We're not getting on the plane." She took his hand and swept down the stairs, being careful not to go so fast as to call attention to herself. Matthew was being led toward the far end of the airport. The thug must have a gun pointed at his back.

Once down the stairs she hurried across the carpet to the exit. "Jamie, Mama needs to take care of something." She bent down and cupped her hands on his cheeks. "Do you remember where Matthew parked the truck?"

He nodded.

"I need you to go back there. Walk, don't run. After you get into the truck, keep your head down below the dashboard. I'll come for you as quickly as I can. No matter what, don't leave the truck."

Again he nodded, his eyes filled with trust. It was a risk to separate from him, but taking him into the violence that might be coming was even riskier. Chances were there wouldn't be any men out in the parking lot—they were all in the terminal looking for her and her son. She knew Corben wanted Jamie. She wouldn't give any of the thugs the opportunity to grab him.

Blondie had been leading Matthew toward a side exit. She ran in that direction. She glanced over her shoulder to see Jamie carefully making his way back to the truck. She exited through the door where Matthew and the thug must have gone. The airport was undergoing some construction and the heavy equipment and supplies were stored here. There would be no traffic through this area. She moved around a pile of steel beams. Her eyes searched for Matthew. Was she too late?

Other than the gusting wind, she couldn't hear anything. She circled around a crane. Where else could they have gone? Rochelle noticed an iron bar on the ground and picked it up. To her left was a field where it looked like out-of-use planes were parked. She saw movement behind one of the planes. Two people walking, one behind the other. She ran in that direction, slowing down as she got closer. Though the body of the plane blocked her view of the men's faces, one of them had dropped to his knees. She recognized Matthew's dark brown pants.

Her heart racing, she circled around to the back of the plane. She had a view of Blondie's back and Matthew on his knees. She raised the metal rod to knock the thug down. He turned at the sound of her footsteps and her blow landed on his shoulder. The hit disoriented but didn't disable the would-be killer. He went back against the airplane and the gun went flying, but he didn't fall to his knees.

Matthew jerked to his feet. The man came after him with his fists raised. Matthew dodged the swing and landed a hit to the man's stomach, which caused him to double over.

Matthew grabbed Rochelle's hand and darted around the plane and back toward the airport. When she glanced over her shoulder, the thug was about forty yards behind them.

Rochelle spoke as she ran. "Jamie is back at your truck."

Matthew headed toward the parking lot. They ducked down behind a compact car for a breather, and to check if they were being followed.

He touched his hand to her cheek, his eyes glowing with affection. "You came back for me."

"It's what you would have done for me." She lifted her head, listening for footsteps.

"Let's get moving." Crouching low, they zigzagged through the parked cars. Matthew lifted his head above the hood of an older-model car to gauge where their pursuer was. "I don't see him." He pressed against her shoulder lightly. "Let's keep going."

Rochelle moved forward, still using the cars to shield her. She stopped, and her breath froze in her throat when she saw Blondie two cars away from them with his back toward them. Matthew did an about-face as they hurried away on all fours.

The man was so close Rochelle feared her heavy breathing would give them away. Her heart pounded in her rib cage. With a backward glance, Matthew pointed in the direction they needed to go. She could see the truck, but not Jamie. She had told him to stay down. Her heart squeezed a little tighter. She hoped that was why she couldn't see him.

They had a stretch of open area to run across to get to the truck. As they rested against the bumper of a car, Rochelle took in a breath and braced herself. Matthew nodded and they took off running.

Though she could not see the thug, a gunshot landed close by, nearly clipping her heels. They were twenty feet from the truck. Her hands reached out for the door handle. When she opened the door, Jamie sat up. Her joy at seeing him was beyond words.

She jumped in, wrapping her arms around Jamie, and Matthew piled in behind her. He fumbled in his pocket for the keys. Through the windshield, she saw the thug stalking straight toward them.

Matthew clicked the key in the ignition and shifted into Reverse. The thug raised his gun, and Rochelle covered Jamie with her body.

Matthew spun the truck around 180 degrees and hit the gas. Within minutes, they had turned onto the road that led to the highway.

"I'll take you out of town. There are other airports in other cities. They can't be watching all of them."

Rochelle sat back in the seat, allowing Jamie to sit up. Her mind raced. How long could this go on? "He found me once. He'll find me again."

Matthew glanced over at her. "What are you saying?"

"I'm saying that I can't keep running. I don't want to do this to Jamie. To uproot him again. We have to find a way to put Elwood Corben in jail."

EIGHT

Matthew glanced in the rearview mirror as he tried to absorb what Rochelle was saying. "There is no record of Dylan Corben even dying. I'm not sure where we'd start."

"We?" she asked.

"Yes, I'll help you. I just don't know how." She had risked her own life to save him. He couldn't abandon her now. "What do we do? Go to Seattle and start snooping around? Get in touch with the police there?"

"I already tried to fly out of here. Besides, word would get back to Elwood if we did that. I told you he had policemen in Seattle on his payroll." Rochelle stared out the windshield. "I have to figure out how he covered up Dylan's death first."

For Elwood to do all that he had done, Matthew knew now that Rochelle was telling the truth about seeing Dylan die. "So where do we go from here?"

"Dylan couldn't just vanish without someone asking questions. He had friends. Elwood must have made up some kind of story," Rochelle said.

"We need internet access, probably at a library, see if there was anything in the Seattle papers or on the net that might help us understand what happened ten years ago." Matthew gripped the wheel and chose his words carefully. "Are you sure Dylan was dead?"

"I didn't take his pulse. Elwood saw me and I had to run." She shuddered. "There was blood all over the floor from where he hit his head. He wasn't moving."

"Sorry to make you think about that," he said. Though he trusted Rochelle, he still couldn't fathom why there was no record of Dylan's death or disappearance.

"It's all right." She turned slightly, staring out the window. "If Dylan didn't die that night, why is Elwood coming after me now?"

"Mom?" Jamie's voice was small and quiet.

"Yeah, baby?" Rochelle responded.

"Does this mean we get to go back to live in our old house and I can build robots with Jace?"

Rochelle glanced nervously at Matthew and then stroked Jamie's head. "I'm going to do my best to make that happen, but we have to put this bad man in jail first."

Matthew was glad for Rochelle's change of heart. It made more sense than looking over her shoulder for the rest of her life.

He read a road sign indicating the distances to various towns. "Let's stay out of Discovery. They will be looking for you there. There are lots of little towns around here with libraries. We only need to pick one."

Rochelle gazed through the windshield. "New Irish isn't too far from here."

"It's settled then. We'll go to New Irish. The place is too small to have a police force, but I'm sure they have a library." He stared at the road up ahead as snow started to fall again. If they found nothing, what then? Given his record of seemingly false alarms, the Discovery police weren't likely to get too excited unless they had something solid to bring them.

As a precaution, he checked the rearview mirror. There wasn't a single car behind them. He took the exit for New Irish and eased onto Main Street. It was the busiest street in the farming community of a couple thousand, but it was still quiet.

"There's the library." Rochelle leaned toward him and pointed through the windshield.

"I'm starving." Jamie rubbed his stomach.

"It has been a long time since we ate," Rochelle said.

He spotted a Chinese restaurant and pulled up beside it. He surveyed the street as they stepped out onto the sidewalk. He still hadn't been able to let go of paranoia that they'd been followed. It didn't seem possible that they could be free of Elwood Corben and his hired muscle.

Jamie clapped his hands. "Hope they have a buffet."

Rochelle laughed. "Jamie loves Chinese."

"I think that's the first time I've heard you laugh." He opened the door so she could step through. She met his gaze. He hadn't noticed the auburn tint to her hair or the specks of gold in her brown eyes before.

His heart beat a little faster as she looked away. As they entered the restaurant, he wondered where they would be now if the circumstances of their lives had been different. What if he had just started up a conversation one day when she'd been in her front yard and he walked by? They might be on their way to a concert or a movie. Just two ordinary people getting to know each other. He was willing to admit an attraction to her. Her gesture of risking her own life at the airport had shifted things for him. She cared about him, too. All the same, there was nothing they could do about the blossoming emotion. It was too late to hope for an ordinary life.

The restaurant was empty except for a college-age couple eating together and an older woman by herself. They paid for the buffet and loaded up their plates. Jamie was still filling his plate when Rochelle and Matthew sat down.

The door jangled, and a man walked in. Rochelle glanced over her shoulder and watched the man for a moment.

"He doesn't look like one of them," Matthew said. "I think we're okay here."

She tapped her fork on the table. "I suppose you're right." The tension he saw in her features did not subside. It would be hard for either of them to let their guard down.

He watched her for a moment while she ate. Her cheeks had a rosy glow that was offset by the creaminess of her skin. She caught him staring and gazed at him with her wide brown eyes surrounded by thick lashes. A faint smile graced her face, and she tilted her head. "What are you thinking?"

His face flushed with heat. "I was thinking that I wished I would have stopped and talked to you those times I saw you in the yard and only said hello."

"Yeah, I thought about that, too. You live a few houses away from me, and it takes all of this to happen for us to get a conversation going." She averted her gaze. Her voice filled with emotion. "You're a good person, Matthew."

When he made the decision to go after her when

the thug took her from the hospital, his thoughts had been about Jamie. He knew what it was like to grow up without a dad. The kid would have no chance if he lost his mom, too.

But now, he felt something deep for Rochelle. As he watched her look off into the distance, he was struck by her beauty and her strength. She'd been a good mom through events that would have defeated a lesser person.

Jamie came and sat down beside Rochelle, his plate heaping with food.

"Are you going to be able to eat all that, buddy?" Matthew said.

Rochelle wrapped an arm around Jamie. "He can really pack it away for such a skinny kid."

Matthew grinned as Jamie stabbed a piece of chicken with a fork. He was such an easygoing kid. Easy to like, easy to be around.

As he took a bite of his sweet-and-sour pork, he allowed himself to pretend that they really were just out for an ordinary lunch and that there was no threat to Jamie or Rochelle. Sun from the window washed them in a warm glow. He relished the melodic sound of Rochelle's laughter as Jamie sang a funny song one of his friends had taught him.

They finished up their meal and walked the short distance to the library, which looked like it used to be a Victorian house. A middle-aged woman with short brown hair and purple glasses sat behind a high counter. Rochelle rushed over to her. "Do you have archives of the Seattle papers going back ten years?"

The woman stood up and scurried around the desk. "We have newspapers from most of the major cities." She walked over to a computer and sat in front of the keyboard. "All the newspaper archives vary as to how far back they go." She tapped the keyboard. "Which city were you interested in again?"

"Seattle." Her voice sounded strained. This was a long shot at best.

The librarian tapped a few more keys.

Jamie leaned close to his mother. "Can I go to the children's section?" He pointed toward a door that was decorated in primary colors.

"Sure, honey." Rochelle was focused on the computer screen as she stood behind the librarian. Matthew stood close to Rochelle while the librarian paged through several screens.

His hand slipped into Rochelle's, and he gave her fingers a supportive squeeze. She turned toward him, her face inches from his as her gaze traveled up and she offered him a faint smile.

The moment warmed him all the way to the bone.

The librarian's voice broke his reverie. "Here we go. Looks like you're in luck. That newspaper goes back about twelve years. Feel free to browse," she said as she scooted the chair back and returned to her counter.

Rochelle sat down and Matthew pulled up a chair beside her. "This is it. I hope we find something helpful."

Rochelle took in a breath. Her stomach clenched as she clicked back through the years and the memories started to flow. Dylan had died in September.

Matthew leaned closer to her to see the screen. His body heat enveloped her and made her light-headed. She'd felt a spark when he'd held her hand. The attraction was not unexpected. He was a good man. But she had thought his commitment to get her to a safe place was being driven by wanting to give Jamie a fighting chance. Maybe there was something more there.

It was hard to gauge her own emotions. They'd been thrown together through such traumatic circumstances. Maybe she was only responding to him out of need, because of the threat of Elwood Corben. After she lost Dylan, her heart had been walled off. She certainly didn't want to experience that pain ever again in any way, so why be open to the possibility of caring for someone?

She couldn't sort through all of it. All she knew was that it felt wonderful to have him so close, to smell the mixture of wood smoke and soap that he exuded.

She drew her attention back to the computer, pulling up the newspaper that came out the day after she saw Dylan killed. Nothing came up when she searched Dylan's name. The days after that yielded similar results. She was six days past the murder and losing hope when she got a hit on Dylan's name. She pulled up an article from the business section. She leaned closer to the computer screen. The article stated that Dylan had taken an overseas job in his father's shipping business. She shook her head. This had to be part of the cover-up.

Matthew read over her shoulder. "Elwood is in shipping?"

She nodded. "Some of it is legitimate. Enough so that no one gets suspicious. But he really makes his living transporting any kind of illegal thing you can imagine. Dylan had just figured it out. He was working in his dad's warehouse when he accidentally dropped a package off the forklift and found some drugs hidden in a sculpture. In the preceding weeks he'd discovered other things that seemed suspicious—artifacts and jewelry packaged in strange ways."

Dylan had been so afraid and angry the night he'd told her what he'd found. His world had been shattered. His father wasn't at all who Dylan thought he was. He was a fraud. She could close her eyes and hear the tremble in his voice as he told her everything. She stanched the flow of memories.

Matthew leaned closer to her. "This is still really hard for you to talk about, isn't it?"

She turned so she was facing him. She saw immense compassion in his eyes. "I guess I haven't thought about it…not since that night."

"Did you love Dylan?"

"Yes, we talked about running away and getting married. He wanted nothing to do with his father." The shame of having been pregnant and not married hit her with full force. "We were just kids." She'd worked through all of this when she'd stayed at the home for pregnant teens. Naomi's Place had been a healing place for her. She'd found her faith again, had asked God's forgiveness and forgave herself, but something about talking to Matthew about this brought up unresolved feelings.

"So much to go through for someone so young. Yet you managed to pull together a life for you and your kid." His voice held no judgment.

She lifted her gaze.

He leaned a little closer to her. As she searched his eyes, she wondered if he was thinking about kissing her.

A fear rose up in her that caused her to jerk back. She didn't want to fall for Matthew only to lose him. That was pain she did not want to revisit in any form. She and

Jamie might not even be able to stay in Discovery. She caught the flicker of disappointment in his expression.

Matthew nodded, but she saw the hurt in his eyes. A moment later, he rose to his feet and wandered around the library.

She did a general internet search for Dylan's name, but came up with nothing.

Jamie came out of the children's section, glanced at his mom and then headed toward the young-adult part of the library. He disappeared around a bookshelf.

A heaviness had descended on the room. Matthew stood with his hands in his pockets, his back turned toward her as he gazed out a high window.

She turned her attention back to the computer screen. The question that had plagued her since Elwood had shown up was what had happened to make him finally hunt her down. Was it possible it had taken him this long to find her?

What she was able to find wasn't really very much information. Rochelle sat back in her chair feeling overwhelmed at the David and Goliath battle in front of her.

A hand rested on her shoulder. "Did you find anything else?"

The heat of Matthew's touch seeped through to her skin.

"I'm trying to figure out why Elwood came for me after ten years." She twisted the necklace she wore.

"We didn't expect to find all the answers. Maybe your eye witness account and what we found out here today will get the ball rolling."

She tensed as old fears returned. "Dylan told me that one of the reasons Elwood was never caught for his illegal transports was that he had some of the Seattle cops on his payroll. I don't think we can go to them. It wouldn't be safe."

"There must be a policeman in Discovery you can trust. You work in the courts. You must know some of them," Matthew said.

She thought for a moment. "There was a detective who testified in a human-trafficking trial recently. His name is Bryan Keyes. He seemed very honest and diligent. He worked really hard to make sure the guy accused of the trafficking got to trial. The investigation was dropped at one point, but he wouldn't give up."

"That's it then. He sounds like our guy. We've got to find a way to make contact with him and set up a meeting."

She shuddered. She wasn't so sure this would work. "But you said the police already have us blacklisted."

"That's why you need to call them. Just be honest about what you found out and what has happened to you here in Discovery. They've got to at least arrest those musclemen who have been coming after you." Matthew grabbed her hand. "You can do this." His gaze was unwavering, "For you and for Jamie."

She found a measure of strength from the pressure of his hand holding hers and the determination she saw in his eyes.

"I'll go get Jamie, and we'll figure things out from there." She stood up and headed toward the young-adult section of the library. She glanced down the three corridors between the bookshelves but didn't find him. She peeked back into the children's room, which was also empty. She saw no other patrons in the library.

By the time she saw the librarian come through a door across the room, her heart was beating fast. Rochelle purged the worry from her voice. "Have you seen my son?"

"Last time I saw him he was over in the YA section. I've been on a conference call for about the past ten minutes."

Matthew came up beside her.

Her pulse drummed in her ears as guilt washed over her. Why had she let her guard down? "I can't find Jamie."

"He's got to be around here somewhere." He directed his question to the librarian. "Is there any place else he could have gone?"

She shook her head. "This is not a big library. The upstairs rooms are not for the public and they are locked."

"Is there a back entrance, and can the public use that?" Rochelle pushed down the rising anxiety.

"Yes and yes." The librarian pointed toward a door on the far side of the room.

From the computer area where they'd been sitting, the view to the second exit was blocked. Someone could have come in here and taken Jamie without them ever seeing it.

"He must have gone outside." Matthew placed a reassuring hand on her back. "We'll look."

Rochelle tried not to give in to panic. They couldn't have been found here. She stepped out onto the street and glanced both ways.

"It's not like him to wander off." She tried to keep her voice calm, but her hands were shaking.

"You walk a few blocks that way. I'll run down and check to see if he went back to the truck." Matthew jogged down the street.

Rochelle crossed her arms against the cold. Her heart pounded against her rib cage and her neck muscles had twisted into a tight knot. She scanned the street, not seeing any sign of Jamie. She walked briskly and then turned back toward the library.

Matthew was waiting for her on the library steps when she returned.

She could not stop the tears from falling. "Where could he have gone?"

Matthew shook his head as worry lines formed on his forehead. "We weren't followed. I checked." His words were tinged with doubt.

Rochelle put a trembling hand over her mouth. She could not go on without her sweet boy. Despair seemed to freeze both of them in place as snow fell around them.

Matthew reached out and drew her into a hug. "We'll find him."

Matthew sounded as if he was about to fall apart, too. She'd underestimated just how much he cared about Jamie.

The door burst open and the librarian stepped out. "He's here, asleep in a room that was supposed to be locked."

Rochelle let out a breath and burst back up the stairs. The librarian led her to a room that looked like it was used for storage. Her little boy was curled up on a bean-bag chair that looked like it needed to be repaired. He clutched a book close to his chest and his glasses rested on a stack of magazines beside him.

Rochelle breathed a sigh of relief. "Let's just let him sleep."

When she looked at Matthew, she saw the glow of

affection for her son in his eyes. He tilted his head back toward the library. "Let's go sit down."

They found a place to sit in two overstuffed chairs that faced each other.

"I was really afraid something had happened to Jamie." Her heart rate was just now returning to normal. She stared out the window at the falling snow and at the little rock garden in the rear yard of the library. The scare confirmed her decision to try to get Elwood in jail. She and Jamie couldn't live like this forever.

Matthew cleared his throat. "Rochelle, what if we could find a safe place for Jamie to stay? Someplace Corben would never think to look for him." His tone was gentle.

"I don't know where that place would be. Elwood managed to figure out who my friend was and where I lived. How could we be sure he wouldn't find Jamie if we hid him somewhere?"

"It would have to be a location they couldn't connect to either of us," Matthew said.

"I don't know if I'm comfortable with that. Protecting Jamie is my job. Being separated from him when I was in the hospital was excruciating. I need to see him at night and know that he is safe."

"I understand. It's not an easy decision to make," he said.

Turmoil and uncertainty made her stomach tighten into a hard ball. Matthew had a point. Was she really looking out for Jamie's safety, or was her decision motivated by her own selfish need? "When I thought that Corben had somehow tracked us down here in New Irish, I saw my life without my little boy and I—" Her throat constricted and she couldn't speak. She put her hand on her mouth.

He reached across the table that was between them and draped his hand over hers. "The same thoughts went through my head."

His touch had a calming effect on her. Even after he pulled his hand away, the warmth of his touch lingered. It was amazing to see how much he cared about Jamie.

Matthew sat back in the chair and stared out the window. "Let's think about what our next move is. We know that Corben is not going to try to kill you until he knows where Jamie is."

Rochelle touched her hand to her chest. "Yes, it seems that way, unless he figures it's not worth the risk waiting around. He might get impatient...and just decide to kill me." The idea caused a shiver to run along her spine.

"I think our first step is to call this local policeman you think might help. You can probably use the library phone to make the call. I doubt there's a place in this town to buy a cell phone."

"I guess I better do this then." She rose to her feet and tracked down the librarian who directed her to a free phone that she could use. Rochelle leafed through the phone book until she found the number for the police station.

This was a gamble in so many ways. She had to hope Detective Keyes would want to help and that he was as honest as he seemed. Even then, she was afraid Elwood would find a way to avoid prosecution. So many obstacles to getting justice lay in front of her.

She took a breath and lifted up the phone.

NINE

Matthew moved to a couch and watched from a distance as Rochelle made her call. He couldn't tell from her expression how the conversation was going.

The door to the storage room opened and Jamie wandered out, rubbing his eyes with his fists.

"Hey, sleepyhead."

Jamie plopped down beside him on the couch. The boy leaned against Matthew. "I got really tired. I miss my room."

He wrapped his arm around Jamie and drew him close. "Understood, buddy."

"What's Mom doing?"

"She's trying to find a way for this bad man not to chase you two anymore."

Jamie laid his head against the back of the couch and let out a heavy breath. "I would like that."

Rochelle hung up the phone and hurried over to them. "Detective Keyes is willing to take my statement. If he feels there is a case, he'll contact a lawyer in Washington. We don't even have to deal with the Seattle police outright. He can meet us in an hour at a picnic area midway between here and Discovery. There's a Lewis and Clark historical marker there."

"I know which one that is," Matthew said. "It won't take us more than twenty minutes to get there."

"You want to do an *I Spy* book while we wait?" Jamie piped up.

Matthew shrugged. "Sure."

Jamie ran to the children's area to retrieve the book.

Rochelle sat down beside him. Her shoulder brushed against his, and he was reminded of the moment they had shared earlier by the computers. He had been drawn to her, tempted to kiss her, but she'd pulled away. Her coldness hurt him, but maybe it was for the best anyway. He couldn't even sort through what the attraction was about anyway. Was it just one more way for him to rescue her?

Rochelle turned to face him. "Thank you for being such a good sport about entertaining Jamie."

"I really don't mind. Jamie is a lot of fun. He's a good kid." And he meant that. He really cared about that boy.

A faint smile graced her face. "Thanks. That's what I've always thought about him."

Jamie returned holding the book. "Let me sit in the middle and then we can all look at it."

They sat for half an hour looking for hidden objects in the *I Spy* pictures. The time passed quickly, and he felt a little disappointed when he looked at the clock and saw it was time to go. Being with Rochelle and Jamie was beginning to feel like the most natural thing in the world. Like they fit together.

Rochelle's expression clouded when she saw him looking at the clock. This was not their life, sitting in a warm library enjoying each other's company. They had to face a much harsher reality.

They walked silently out to the truck and got back in. He started the engine and eased out of the parking space.

"I hope this works." Rochelle's voice came out monotone, as though she wasn't willing to commit an emotional response to what they were about to do.

A little doubt crept into his mind, as well. "Me, too." What else could they do? Their backs were up against a wall, and they were out of choices.

Matthew stared through the windshield. The roads had gotten a little icier since they'd come to New Irish.

The miles clicked by without anyone speaking, till finally Matthew broke the silence. "Did you ask Detective Keyes about protection for you and Jamie?"

"He knows I'm connected to you. He knows about the calls you made to the station that came across as false alarms, but he's willing to listen to me." She stared out the window. "I think that is the most we can ask for now."

He watched the landmarks along the road, feeling a rising tension in his muscles. Maybe it was Rochelle telling him about Elwood being in the habit of having cops on his payroll. He hoped Elwood couldn't have managed something like that in Discovery.

Matthew slowed the truck. The picnic area was hidden from view of the road by a thick grove of trees. There were no other cars when they pulled into the area.

"Can we go over and read the historical marker?" Jamie asked, leaning forward.

"I think we should wait here in the truck." Rochelle glanced at her watch. "We're right on time."

Matthew killed the engine as the snow drifted out of the sky.

"Can't we listen to the radio or something?" Jamie's voice held a note of anxiety.

"No, we just have to wait," Rochelle said. Another ten minutes passed.

Jamie wiggled in his seat.

Something was beginning to feel very wrong. Matthew fiddled with the keys. "Maybe we should go."

"He might have gotten delayed. We don't have cell phones, so there's no way he can reach us," Rochelle said.

He scanned the area around the truck and out toward the surrounding forest. "How long do you think we should wait?"

"This is the best shot we have at putting Elwood in jail. Let's give it a couple more minutes at least," Rochelle said.

Jamie started to sing the same silly song he'd sung earlier.

"Jamie, please, be quiet." Her tone revealed the stress she must be feeling.

A truck pulled into the lot through the same entrance they had used.

"That must be him," said Matthew.

"Who's that guy?" Jamie pointed in the other direction where an SUV had parked while they were focused on the truck.

Adrenaline kicked Matthew's heartbeat up a notch. They'd been set up.

Terror shot through Rochelle. "It's an ambush. We have to get out of here."

"They're blocking both exits." Matthew angled his head from side to side as he shifted into gear.

"Mom, I'm scared. What's happening?"

Rochelle wrapped her arm around Jamie.

The door of the first truck opened, and a man stepped out, stalking toward them. She recognized him as one of the thugs they'd encountered earlier.

Matthew spun the car around and headed toward an open patch of ground where there were no trees.

The man ran back to his truck and jumped in. The SUV with the dark windows did not move, blocking the other exit. The other car burst toward them. Matthew hit Reverse while spinning in a half circle and zoomed toward the open exit. They clipped the side-view mirror of the truck as they sped by it.

When he turned onto the main road, the SUV had moved to block the road back to New Irish. He spun around again and headed back toward Discovery.

With her arms still wrapped around Jamie, who had started to cry, Rochelle looked out the back window. "They're both behind us."

"We have no choice. We gotta go back to Discovery." Matthew gripped the steering wheel and increased his speed.

Rochelle tensed as she watched the speedometer needle moving. Going this fast on icy roads could have dangerous consequences.

As Jamie continued to sob, Rochelle soothed him. "How could this happen? How did they find out?"

"Maybe Detective Keyes isn't the honest man you thought he was." Matthew stared straight ahead.

The sound of Jamie's crying cut right through her. She hated that her son had to suffer for her choices. All she ever wanted to do was protect him.

"Looks like we lost one of them."

Rochelle glanced over her shoulder where the truck had spun in the road and was headed toward a ditch. "They've made it so we have to head back to Discovery."

"We're certainly more vulnerable there." Matthew put more distance between them and the SUV with dark windows. Twice his truck fishtailed, but Matthew corrected and the truck stayed on the road. They rounded several curves and then came out on a straight stretch of road.

The other car was still behind them but just a speck in the rearview mirror.

"What are you going to do now?" Rochelle gripped the dashboard.

Jamie had stopped crying but still looked pale and distraught. She'd give anything for him not to have to go through this.

"We don't have a lot of choices." He glanced down at the gauges. "We're almost out of gas."

Her stomach tightened, and she could not shake off the rising anxiety. "We have to stop. Can't we turn off somewhere? I don't want to go back to Discovery."

"There'll be a gas station before we have to go all the way back there. We might be able to shake these guys before then."

Though she appreciated Matthew's optimism, she wasn't so sure about that.

Road signs came up advertising a one-horse town with limited services. Matthew hit the blinker. The other car was still visible behind them.

The gas station was the first thing they encountered

when they got off the exit. Matthew clicked open the door. "You two just stay in the truck. This will only take a minute."

Rochelle placed a protective arm around Jamie as she kept up a vigil of looking out each window. She could hear Matthew fumbling with the gas nozzle. He tapped on the window, and she rolled it down.

"There's something wrong with the pump. I'm going to have to go inside and get some help."

Her gaze darted around. The only other pump was already being used. "We should go with you then."

"That probably would be best." He opened the passenger-side door.

"I don't like this." Fear colored Jamie's words.

"I know, honey." She held him close as they walked toward the service station. Matthew's gaze never stopped moving. Inside, two other customers waited in line for the only clerk.

Rochelle tensed. No car resembling the SUV that chased them pulled into the station. Yet, she couldn't help but feel the clock was ticking. The station was visible from the road. They couldn't hope that the SUV would just whiz by and not backtrack. They needed to get out of here fast.

Matthew leaned on the counter and addressed the clerk even though the two people were still in line. "I'm having trouble with that pump and we're in kind of a hurry."

The clerk, a short man with a buzz cut, offered him a genuine smile. "I'll get to you as soon as I can, sir."

The two people waiting in line gave Matthew a dirty look. The clerk finished with the second customer and then got into a conversation about weather while he rang up an older woman's purchases.

A rope of tension tightened around Rochelle's torso while they waited. She drew Jamie closer. Finally, the older woman said her goodbye and headed toward the door.

The clerk grabbed a winter hat from under the counter. "Trouble with the pump, huh?"

In the time they had waited for the clerk, the driver at the second pump had pulled away and another had taken his place.

Matthew said, "I can't get it to zero out or start."

"It's tricky sometimes." The clerk came around from behind the counter. "I'll see if I can get it to work."

Impending doom seemed to settle over them like a heavy blanket. This had taken too long already.

Matthew's compressed features revealed that he was feeling the same level of anxiety. "Why don't you two get back in the cab? We'll deal with this."

Once they were outside, she pulled open the passenger-side door. "Jamie, you can get in first." Her voice came out as a harsh whisper. She glanced from side to side before getting in herself.

She focused on the sound of Matthew and the clerk talking and the nozzle being put in the gas tank. She breathed a sigh of relief when she looked over and saw the numbers racing by on the gallons' and dollars' readouts.

A moment later, Matthew got into the truck.

She took in the first deep breath she'd taken since they'd pulled into the gas station. Matthew turned the key in the ignition. The engine didn't turn over. He tried a second time with the same result.

Matthew's words had a cold edge to them. "Looks like we have truck trouble."

Rochelle's heart squeezed tight. This couldn't be happening.

TEN

Matthew let out a heavy breath as an idea played at the corners of his mind. What if the truck had had some help in not running? Maybe the sabotage was intended to make them break down on the lonely country road and they'd gotten lucky. Their view of the far side of the truck had been completely obstructed in the five or so minutes they'd waited inside.

"We need to push the truck away from the pump so people can get gas if they need to," he told Rochelle.

"I can steer," she said.

"I'll need your help pushing." He cupped Jamie's shoulder. "Jamie my man, do you think you can handle steering?"

For the first time since they'd been chased, Jamie's expression brightened. "Really? That's, like, a grown-up job."

They pushed the truck off to the side, and Matthew flipped open the hood. His mechanical knowledge was limited. Nothing obvious was wrong, no disconnected hoses or missing caps on anything.

The clerk came outside and stood beside him. "Got car trouble, huh?"

"Yeah, does this garage work on cars?" Matthew asked.

The clerk shook his head. "No, we're a small operation. The best I can do is arrange to have it towed into Discovery."

"Back to Discovery. That's our only choice." Matthew glanced over at Rochelle and Jamie, who rested on the bench outside the gas station. He saw the fear in her eyes with the mention of Discovery.

"You can ride in with the tow truck driver." The clerk's voice had a forced cheerfulness to it. "Sorry I can't do more."

"Give us a minute," Matthew said. "That's probably what we'll have to do."

He walked over to Rochelle. She drew her eyebrows together. He could only guess at the anxiety she was feeling. "I don't want to go back there."

"I know, but what choice do we have?" He straightened up and glanced around. "We both know that truck didn't break down all by itself. If we're left here without a vehicle, we're sitting ducks."

Her gaze had become a bit unfocused as she hugged Jamie a little tighter. "I think maybe we should go back to the first plan and leave the state."

"That's not really a viable option right now. I don't have a way to get you to an airport or a bus station. You know in your heart that's not what you want. You want this to be over once and for all."

She ran her fingers through her long hair. "But we tried to make Elwood pay for his crimes and look what happened."

"Do you think Detective Keyes is honest? Or do you think Elwood would have gotten to him?"

She shook her head. "I don't know what to think."

"Just because of what happened doesn't mean he's doing Elwood's bidding. The phones could be bugged. Another cop who is dirty could have overheard him."

She looked up at him, her eyes filled with desperation. "Maybe we should give him a second chance."

"I don't know yet." Matthew paced back and forth. "Your impression of him was that he was honest and a good cop. Let's focus on getting a truck that runs."

The clerk leaned out of the door of the gas station. "Do you want me to call that tow truck or not?"

Rochelle sat up a little straighter, twisting her hair nervously. "Call the tow truck." Her voice held a tone of resolve and strength.

She scooted over on the bench so Matthew could sit down. The little town where they were consisted of the gas station and a post office. A short distance away were a few trailers and houses. Across the road were huge piles of dirt, gravel and moving equipment.

There wasn't a huge amount of traffic through the gas station and he hadn't seen any sign of life in the houses down the road. Still, he felt exposed without a truck for a quick escape. Rochelle went inside to get some cocoa for them. They sipped the hot beverage and waited as the sky grew darker.

The tow truck pulled up and they all squeezed into the cab of the truck. The driver was a burly man with a mop of black hair who laughed at his own jokes.

As they rolled down the road, Matthew's view behind him was obstructed by his truck and the towing equipment. Rochelle sat closest to the door. He noticed her checking the side-view mirror. The worried look never melted from her face.

He reached over and slipped his hand in hers, hoping she would understand the gesture was to ease her anxiety.

The tow truck driver, who said his name was Andy, continued to tell stories that only he found funny. Matthew was grateful he didn't have to contribute much to the conversation. Fatigue had set in.

Rochelle's hand felt warm and silky in his. He couldn't imagine where their lives would end up in the next hour, let alone in a week or two. He might be putting her and Jamie on a bus or plane after all. He didn't like the thought of that. He was growing fond of both of them, but if it was the only way they could be safe...

Rochelle squeezed his hand back and leaned into him. His heart warmed at the gesture. No, he didn't know if she would even be living in Discovery when this was all over. What they had was this moment. He would relish it and not expect more.

The sky grew dark as the taller buildings of the college campus in Discovery came into view. Rochelle tensed beside him. The tow truck driver pulled into a repair garage. Judging from the lack of lights, the place had closed hours ago.

"This is the end of the line, folks."

Matthew faced the tow truck driver. "I have a friend I can call to come get us if we could use your cell phone."

After he handed Matthew his phone, the tow truck driver unhooked the truck.

Though they could see the lights of the city, the garage they had been taken to was on the edge of town with some distance between it and other businesses.

Matthew dialed his friend Daniel. "Hey, listen, I've got a favor to ask of you."

"What's up with you? You didn't show up for your last two shifts."

"I know, but I have a really good reason. Listen, I need you to come get me and two other people up at—" He looked around for the sign. "Leroy's garage."

Daniel must have picked up on the urgency in his voice because he didn't ask any further questions. "Sure, I know the place. I can be there in ten minutes."

Matthew handed the phone to Andy, who waved goodbye as he climbed back into his truck.

"That man sure can talk," said Jamie as he watched the tow truck pull out of the lot.

Both Rochelle and Matthew laughed. Jamie's remark seemed to lighten the moment.

Matthew said, "He was quite the storyteller, wasn't he?"

"I'm really hungry," said Jamie.

Matthew was suddenly aware of his own empty stomach. Other than the cocoa they had while they were waiting, they hadn't eaten anything since the Chinese buffet.

Car headlights appeared up the road. Rochelle grabbed Jamie's hand and shrank back into the shadows underneath the building's eaves. Matthew eased toward them as the car zoomed by.

"Our ride will be here soon enough," Matthew said. If they'd been followed, it seemed like the guy or guys would have made an appearance by now. Maybe the truck breaking down was just an accident.

Rochelle let out a heavy breath. "Where are we even going to stay tonight? They know my friends. They know where your sister lives. They probably know who your friends are, too."

"Elwood and those four or five guys can't be everywhere at once," Matthew said.

After a long heavy silence, Rochelle spoke up. "Jamie, can I talk to Matthew alone?"

"Sure, Mom."

She pulled Matthew off to one side. "I've been thinking about what you said about finding a safe place for Jamie. After what he went through with those men chasing us, I agree. There is one place I know about. The home I stayed in when Jamie was born. It's called Naomi's Place. That was ten years ago. Elwood would never link it back to me."

He'd seen local TV ads for the home in Discovery that took in pregnant teenagers. The information had given him a glimpse into Rochelle's life ten years ago. "That might be an option then. It's late now. Maybe in the morning we can go over there. You and I can figure out our next move."

"Our next move. What choice do we have at this point?" She stepped back closer to Jamie and wrapped her arms around him.

"Maybe we should give Detective Keyes another shot. If we met with him face-to-face in a safe place… maybe we could tell if he was being straight with us." He knew he was grasping at straws, but they had to try to do something.

"If we knew how Elwood found out about our meeting with Detective Keyes, that would help." Rochelle's words landed softly on his ears.

His thoughts raced through the possibilities of their next move. He felt a sense of futility about the situation, but he kept his frustration to himself.

A silence settled around them as they waited in the

shadows, both of them watching the road, waiting for the headlights that meant they had found yet another short reprieve.

"He should be here any minute now." Had he lost all sense of time because of how exposed he felt out here or was Daniel seriously late?

"What's that?" Jamie pointed toward the edge of the property where broken cars were parked.

Matthew heard an odd noise, but he couldn't see anything out in the darkness.

Behind him, Rochelle gasped.

In that moment, he realized what the noise had been—a car door slamming. Two men emerged from the shadows, their forms separating from the darkness.

They must have killed their lights and moved into place earlier, waiting until the tow truck driver had gone.

He grabbed Rochelle's hand just as she pulled Jamie close. "Run, now."

Rochelle's heart pounded. The three of them sprinted away from the men toward the rows of cars and piles of car parts that occupied the other side of the garage. The men's footfalls thundered on the concrete as they closed in on their prey.

Matthew led them away from the outdoor lights by the garage. He moved into a crouch, and she followed suit, making sure Jamie stayed in between them. He checked a car door, but it was locked. Was he looking for a place to hide or a vehicle that could get them out of here?

The men's low, guttural voices drew nearer.

He stuck his hand through a car that had a broken

window and eased the door open. "Get in here." He directed them.

"Where are you going?"

"Being a decoy," he said.

She had no time to protest before he disappeared. She and Jamie crawled into the backseat of the car. She listened to Matthew's fading footsteps. The thug's voices grew louder and more excited. They must have spotted Matthew. She cringed.

The silence fell around them as the seconds ticked by. Jamie pressed close to her, and she could feel him shaking. If they got out of this alive, she'd take him to Naomi's Place until this was over. An innocent child didn't need to witness all of this.

A cold breeze floated in through the broken window, bringing with it the sound of a single gunshot. Both she and Jamie jumped.

Oh, dear God, don't let Matthew be hit.

They waited for what seemed like a hundred years. She heard a voice coming from far away, someone shouting Matthew's name. Fear made her breath catch in her throat. That must be Daniel.

She squeezed her eyes shut as both her hands balled into fists.

Daniel didn't deserve to come to harm.

Daniel's shouting continued a few more times and then the silence surrounded them again. She listened for the sound of a car starting up but didn't hear anything.

Footsteps sounded, and she could see the outline of a man standing close to the car. She crouched down more into the darkness of the floor of the backseat. Jamie sucked in air, and she held her breath while the man paced back and forth just outside the car.

A voice shouted something indiscernible from far away, and the man by the car took off running.

She and Jamie remained still for several minutes, not hearing anything. How long should they wait? She pictured Matthew lying bleeding on the snowy ground, unable to move or come to them. She closed her eyes against that image. She didn't know anything for sure.

"Mom." Though he was inches from her, she could barely hear Jamie. "My hands are really cold."

She positioned her head close to his ear and whispered, "Let's wait a little longer." She reached out and sandwiched his icy hands between her own. He must have left his gloves in the tow truck or dropped them when they were running.

More footsteps pounded, and then Matthew's face appeared at the window. "Daniel's waiting on the other side of the yard down the street."

The strain in his voice made his words come out garbled.

She pushed the door open and stepped out after Jamie. "What happened to those men?"

"I threw them off, but we don't have much time."

Matthew led them through the maze of cars away from the lights of the garage. When they stepped out onto the street, she noticed he bent forward as he jogged.

Up ahead, she saw a car parked on an empty street. The engine was running and the lights were on. Matthew glanced over his shoulder. "We got to hurry."

She didn't dare look to see what was behind them. Matthew opened the back door for them, and they crawled into the passenger seat. Daniel sped away before she'd even pulled the door shut.

When she gazed through the back window, one of the thugs was on the sidewalk running toward them.

They got to the part of town where there were more buildings and streetlights. As the lights blazed into the car she saw now why Matthew had run bent over. He gripped his arm where blood had soiled his coat.

"Matthew, you're hurt." She leaned forward and touched his shoulder. The coat fabric was torn.

"I scraped against some sharp metal when I was trying to hide."

Daniel piped up. "It's just a scratch. We'll take him back to my place and fix him up. He'll be all right."

Judging from the pain she saw reflected on Matthew's face, it wasn't just a scratch.

"Won't they find us at Daniel's place?" she asked Matthew.

"It's a chance we have to take. Daniel's the only one I trust to fix this cut."

Daniel said, "I'll make sure we're not followed. I'll do so many zigs and zags they won't be able to track us."

They had a decent head start. It didn't look like anyone was behind them.

"We'll get out of there as quickly as we can, Rochelle." Matthew spoke through gritted teeth.

And go where and do what?

She gave in to the despair she'd been beating down since the ambush at the picnic site. Had she been a fool to think she could take down someone like Elwood Corben?

Daniel kept his word and wove through several residential neighborhoods before stopping in front of some condos. Once they were inside the garage, Rochelle got out first so she could help Matthew from his seat. She saw the strain on his face as he eased to his feet. The bloodstain had grown larger. He offered her a smile that was totally fake, an effort on his part to ease the anxious look he probably saw on her face.

"You don't have to pretend you're all right." She lifted his uninjured arm and rested it across her back and on her shoulder.

"Guess we're even now. I took care of you when you were injured." His words came between gasps.

"No, I think you're three or four up on that score for all you've done for me," she said.

Daniel unlocked his door, and they entered the living room of the condo. Jamie trudged in looking as though he had gone numb inside. His face was drained of color and his expression was neutral.

"Rochelle, you want to take Matt to the kitchen and get him in a chair?" Daniel said. "Get that coat and shirt off him so we can deal with the wound."

Rochelle watched Jamie a moment longer, her concern over what he'd witnessed growing deeper with each incident.

Daniel touched Jamie's shoulder. "Hey, buddy, you like video games? I got a pretty cool setup here." Daniel opened the doors of his television console, revealing his game system.

Jamie's face brightened. "Wow."

The tension around her torso let up a little bit. He was resilient, just another character quality to admire about her son. Rochelle listened to Daniel explain how the game system worked while she helped Matthew into the kitchen. She lowered him onto a chair. He, too, looked pale but for a different reason.

She touched his shoulder. "Daniel said we needed to take your coat and shirt off."

"You can just cut the sleeve off. It's not like I want to save bloodstained clothes."

She searched the drawers and came up with a pair of kitchen shears. "This should do the job."

She cut as far away from the wound as she could, peeling back the layer of coat fabric and then cutting into the shirt. He winced when her finger grazed over the cut.

"Sorry." She sucked air through her teeth as empathy pain shot through her body.

He gazed at her, his eyes filled with warmth. "It's all right, Rochelle."

"I guess you're more of the expert at this than I am."

"You have a pretty soft touch," he said appreciatively.

When she saw the look in his eyes, something shifted on her emotional landscape. She was drawn to him, but the old fear never went away. She had loved Dylan. All the pain over losing him had served as a barricade around her heart. She hadn't wanted to love again because she didn't want to lose a man again.

"Everything okay? You got kind of a faraway look in your eyes." Matthew's voice was soft, like wind rushing over grass.

"I'm fine." She refocused on cutting his shirtsleeve off. She took in a sharp breath at the sight of his wound. "It's a pretty good-size gash."

Daniel came into the room holding a plastic box with a handle. He set it on the table and flipped it open. "You want to be my lovely assistant?"

"I'll do what I can." Rochelle stared down at the box filled with medical supplies.

"Looks like most of the bleeding has stopped. Let's get this thing sutured. But first we need to disinfect it."

As instructed, Rochelle handed Daniel the disinfectant. Matthew's face tightened from the pain, and his mouth became a hard, straight line.

"Now, I need you to hold the edges of the wound together while I put the suture strips in place."

"Won't that hurt Matthew?"

"Yes, he'll probably cry like a baby." Daniel's tone was playful.

"Yeah, right. You wish." Matthew shot back.

Appreciating the way the banter lightened the moment, Rochelle placed her fingers above and below the wound. She watched Matthew's face, gauging how much pain he was in as she drew the edges of skin together. His biceps muscle stiffened, and he sat up straighter, but he didn't make a sound.

Daniel finished and wrapped a gauze bandage around Matthew's muscular arm. "If you want to go check the medicine cabinet in the bathroom, I think I have some Tylenol in there."

Rochelle walked through the living room on her way to the bathroom.

Jamie looked up from the game he was playing. "Hey, Mom."

The love she felt for her son welled up inside her. She rushed over to him and gave him a hug. "I'm so sorry for everything that has happened. I was only trying to keep you safe."

His little hand patted her back. "Mom, it's okay."

"I don't want us to have to live like this anymore." She pulled away from the hug. "I promise I will do everything in my power to make that happen." She touched her hand to his cheek. Even as she spoke she wondered how she could do that.

He nodded, but there was a weariness in his eyes that she hadn't seen before. She hugged him again as regret washed over her. If only Dylan hadn't died that night. Maybe they could have gotten away and been a family. She returned to the kitchen.

"Got some enchiladas heating up in the microwave. There's plenty if you and Jamie want some," Daniel said.

"Thanks." After Daniel's and Matthew's plates were done, she found two plates and dished up food from the casserole dish.

She placed one of the dishes in the microwave.

Daniel got up. "I'll go see if I can find an air mattress to set up in the living room. Matt, you can have the couch." He left the room.

Seeing that look in Jamie's eyes was the final nail in the coffin of her thinking she could take on Elwood Corben. "I'm thinking that maybe Jamie and I should leave town. I think the eastbound bus leaves at seven in the morning."

Matthew shook his head as though he could not accept what she was saying. "What about taking Jamie to Naomi's Place? So you and I can work on this together."

While she waited for the food to heat up, she felt the weight of Matthew's gaze on her. When she glanced at him, she couldn't quite read what she saw in his eyes.

"Are you sure this is what you want to do? Give up and leave town."

She closed her eyes. "What other choice do I have? You saw what happened when I tried to find justice where Elwood Corben was concerned. I can't beat him, and it's killing me to see what Jamie has been through."

"I understand how you feel. It just seems wrong that he gets to walk around a free man after all that he's done." Matthew used his fork to push his food around his plate.

She took the plate of hot food out of the microwave, placed the next one in and reheated it. She shook her head. "You know, when Detective Keyes agreed to meet us, I actually thought maybe I could end this nightmare, and I would be able to talk to my family again. I haven't heard my mother's voice in ten years. She's never seen Jamie." Her throat went tight from the pain of all of it. "She doesn't even know she has a grandchild."

He rose to his feet and rubbed her back. "I wish you didn't have to go."

"Me, too." He seemed to finally accept her decision. She turned to face him, getting lost in the depth of his eyes. She knew now what emotion she had seen on his face earlier, the deep affection he had for her.

He leaned in and kissed her delicately on the lips. In the next room, Daniel was making Jamie laugh.

Both of them pulled away, though the heat of his touch lingered on her lips.

She realized that the hardest part about leaving town was not that Elwood Corben would still be walking free—it was that she would miss Matthew and never know what might have developed between them.

After everyone had eaten, Matthew fell asleep on the couch. Rochelle lay down on the air mattress with Jamie, but only until he fell asleep. She got up and paced the living room.

Light from outside fell across the couch where Matthew slept. Daniel had loaned him a fresh T-shirt, and the blanket was pulled up to the middle of his chest. He turned over on his injured arm and groaned in pain.

She stared out the window. The snow had a blue cast to it from the streetlights. Like an elephant sitting on her chest, the heaviness of uncertainty made it hard to breathe.

As she watched the heavy snowfall outside, she wondered if she was doing the right thing.

ELEVEN

Matthew jerked awake when a sharp pain traveled down his arm. He got up and found the Tylenol still sitting on the table where Rochelle had left it. He poured himself a drink of water and took another pill. Through the kitchen window, he saw that it was still dark outside and snowing heavily. The clock on the stove said it was five in the morning. In another two hours, he'd be saying goodbye to Rochelle and Jamie.

The kiss last night had not been impulsive. He wanted her to know how he felt even if he would never see her again. Her hand had rested on his chest for a moment when he leaned down to kiss her. He was struck by the bittersweetness of that touch. She'd never again press her hand against his heart and feel it beating. And he'd never smell her honey-scented skin.

He closed his eyes and rubbed the area between his eyebrows. It was what it was. He couldn't change it. They couldn't even complete the first step of finding an honest cop who believed them, let alone put a case together against Corben. She was probably right about needing to leave town. Why did it feel as if he was in a perpetual state of saying goodbye to her?

He showered while the others slept. When everyone else was getting cleaned up, he made bacon, eggs and toast for them.

Rochelle came into the kitchen, her long brown hair still wet from the shower. "Wow, this looks like quite a feast."

Her tone was so formal, as though she were already trying to put emotional distance between the two of them.

"Thought you'd like a hardy breakfast. Kind of hard to find good food on a long bus ride."

She didn't respond, but he thought he saw sorrow in her eyes.

Daniel bounded into the kitchen. "Whoa, someone's been busy. Chef Matthew is in the house."

"It's the least I can do for you after all you've done for us." He patted Daniel on the back.

They ate the meal, talking about things that didn't matter. From time to time, he caught Rochelle watching him. So much was going unsaid between them, and it would never be spoken. If only they had more time.

Matthew warmed up Daniel's car. Jamie got into the back and Rochelle sat beside Matthew in the passenger seat. A snowplow went by on the street.

"It snowed a lot last night," Matthew said. The comment seemed shallow. Was the weather the only safe thing they could talk about?

When they got out to a main street, the snowplows had piled the snow high enough so that it formed a wall on either side of the street. Traffic was light at this hour.

"Are the buses even going to be running?" Rochelle's voice sounded strained.

Matthew clicked on the radio. They were three

blocks away from the bus station when a news report about the storm finally came on. The major highways going out of Discovery were closed and not expected to be cleared for at least a day or more.

Rochelle let out a heavy breath and placed her face in her hands. "What now?"

"It's not that bad. We just have to find a place for you to stay until the roads open up. A hotel or something."

Matthew checked the rearview mirror.

He thought he'd seen a white van following them while he made several turns. But it was a dark sedan behind him now. If Corben had followed them to Daniel's house, it made more sense for him to make a move last night.

"It better be a cheap motel. I have to save my money for when we get to where we're going. It'll take time to find a job and a place to live." Her voice filled with frustration.

"I have some money saved. I can help you out with that," Matthew said.

"No, Matthew, you've done enough." She laced her fingers together and stared down at them.

Her mood had been sullen since they'd left the house.

He drove through the city streets past abandoned cars of people who had foolishly tried to get out ahead of the plows. The scene was a little bit like something from an end-of-the-world movie. Beside him, Rochelle stared straight ahead. A heavy tension had settled in the car. This was a setback she didn't need. Though he was grateful to have a little more time with her, he understood how this must have dashed any hope she had of finally escaping Elwood's grasp.

Jamie spoke up from the backseat. "I have to go to the bathroom."

"That is a problem I can solve," said Matthew. They were still in the residential part of town. He veered toward where he knew there were more businesses and maybe a convenience store.

He spotted a convenience store that had no patrons at all, not even at the gas pumps. The one car parked by the store probably belonged to the clerk. "With a storm this bad, people probably decided to stay home."

He pulled the car up to the door, and they all got out. Rochelle wrapped an arm around Jamie as they stepped into the store. No clerk occupied the area behind the counter.

Rochelle lifted her head above the shelves of merchandise. "I think the bathroom is in the back." Jamie darted toward where she pointed, disappearing behind a potato chip rack.

Rochelle fidgeted with the zipper of her ski jacket. Her jawline indicated tension. She was still upset about the delay in leaving town.

He'd do anything to cheer her up. "You're going to get on that bus." Matthew edged closer to her. "This is just a setback. It's not a catastrophe."

"Yeah, but two days of dodging him..." She put her hand over her mouth and shook her head. "I'm just so tired. I've been dealing with this for ten years."

He rubbed her back, and she leaned against him.

Matthew looked at the shelves of candy. "Guess we should buy something if we're going to use the bathroom. That's the accepted custom, right?"

"How are we going to pay for it with no clerk?" Rochelle walked a short ways down a far aisle, searching.

"The store is open. He must be around here somewhere." Matthew walked toward a back exit and pushed the door open. "I see what's going on." He turned back toward Rochelle. "He's trying to help a lady who's stuck in the snow. I'll go give them a hand."

Rochelle called out, "We'll meet you back at the car."

He gave her a backward glance, hoping to see her smile, but the look on her face was pensive, as though she were still trying to work through having to stay in Discovery.

Matthew ran outside, and the door slammed behind him.

While Rochelle waited for Jamie, another customer, an older man, came into the store. He walked halfway down an aisle and then looked toward the checkout counter, his forehead wrinkled.

His confusion warranted an explanation. Rochelle said, "The clerk is outside helping someone who's stuck in the snow."

"Ahh," said the old man. "This snow is something, isn't it? I haven't seen a blizzard like this since the seventies."

"It's the worst I remember since I moved here ten years ago. I was hoping to leave town today," Rochelle said.

Another customer, a man with his billed cap pulled down over his face, came into the store and stalked toward the back wall. Rochelle hadn't gotten a good look at him before he slipped out of view.

The old man rocked toe to heel. "They'll have those passes cleared out in no time."

"I hope so." Her response was halfhearted. Her mind really wasn't on the weather.

The old man checked his watch. "I can't wait around for this guy." He wandered toward the store entrance. "I'm going to a different store."

Rochelle looked toward the back. Jamie should be done by now. A tinge of anxiety caused her stomach to clench. As she moved down the aisle, she didn't see any sign of the other customer who had come in while she was talking to the old man.

She knocked on the bathroom door. "Jamie?" No response.

She turned the knob. The door was unlocked. The air froze in her lungs when she saw that there was no one inside.

"Jamie." She wheezed in air as the fear she'd felt when they'd lost him at the library returned full force.

Her vision blurred. She turned toward the back door where Matthew was.

"Surprise!" Jamie jumped out from behind the potato chip display.

"Jamie, don't ever do that again." Her voice sounded angry, but she hugged him and nearly cried at the same time.

Jamie's lower lip puckered out. "You were just so sad. I was trying to make you laugh."

"Oh, honey, I'm sorry. I became really afraid for a minute." She hugged him tighter. "Let's go back to the car. Matthew is helping someone get their car unstuck."

"He's always helping someone," Jamie said as he fell in step beside his mother.

"Yes, he's like that, isn't he?"

"I like him a lot. He's nice." His voice glowed with affection.

As she opened the door, another shift took place inside her. This barricade around her heart hurt Jamie, too. He was going to grow up, become a teenager. She couldn't teach him how to be a man. Matthew couldn't do that either if they left town.

"I like him a lot, too," she said.

As they stepped out onto the sidewalk, she noticed a van was parked beside Daniel's car. The door to the van slid open and one of the Elwood's thugs jumped out. Rochelle screamed and wrapped her good arm around Jamie, preparing to retreat back into the store. She pushed Jamie behind her, and the thug lunged at them. He grabbed Rochelle's wrist and jerked her away from Jamie.

"Run, Jamie."

The boy dashed into the store. A second thug jumped out of the van to race after her son while the first yanked on her hair. She grabbed her head protectively as her scalp burned.

Out on the street, a car slowed down as the driver stared at them. The man let go of her hair but clamped a hand around her wrist.

"Don't you dare scream." He lifted his coat slightly, revealing a gun.

She could only watch as the car sped up and moved out of view.

The thug yanked her toward the van. She was powerless against his strength. He tossed her inside, and she hit the hard metal surface of the van floor. The impact caused pain to flare through her rib cage and arm. The man jumped in after her and slid the door shut.

She crab walked backward to get away from him. He grabbed her ankle and pulled a length of rope out of his back pocket. She managed to kick him once before he flipped her over and tied her hands together behind her back. As she felt the fabric of a gag being placed in her mouth, she knew her life was over. Her only prayer was that Jamie fared better.

TWELVE

Getting the older woman's car unstuck from the snow had proved more of a task than either Matthew or the clerk had anticipated. As he watched the car pull away, he felt good about what they had been able to do for someone in need.

The clerk patted him on the back. "Thanks, man."

The back door he had come out of burst open, and Jamie ran out. "Matthew!"

Even at a distance, Matthew could see the terror on the boy's face. He ran toward him. The door swung open again and one of Elwood's thugs emerged holding a gun.

Just as Jamie ran into Matthew arms, the thug slipped on the ice, landing on his back. The gun fell out of his hand and spun out of reach across an icy patch.

Matthew pushed Jamie behind him and scrambled to pick up the gun. He pointed it at the thug as he got to his feet. The thug shook his head and ran back around to the front of the building.

"Where's your mother?"

Jamie pointed to where the thug had run.

"Stay with him." Matthew tilted his head toward

the clerk. With the gun still in his hand, he sprinted around the corner just in time to see the thug jump into the passenger seat.

Fear seized his heart. Rochelle was in there. As the van backed up, he ran toward it, grabbed on to the side mirror and banged on the window with the gun. The gun flew out of his hand as the van gained speed and headed toward the street. His arm muscles strained. He knew he couldn't hold on much longer. The menacing face of Rochelle's kidnapper taunted him as he fell off and landed in a snowbank.

Jamie and the clerk came around the corner of the building. Jamie ran toward him as the clerk went back into the store. Matthew rose to his feet.

"Where's my mom? Where is she?"

Matthew shook his head.

Jamie's face turned red. Even as tears streamed down the boy's face, his voice filled with rage. "Why didn't you stop them?"

"I tried, buddy." His throat constricted from the sympathy welling up inside him. His heart ached for what might become of Rochelle. He would never forgive himself. Why hadn't he just stayed close to them?

Jamie slammed against him so hard he almost fell over. At first, the boy beat his fists against Matthew's chest, but gradually he hugged Matthew and sobbed.

He'd seen the van make a turn, and he knew it was moving slowly because of the snow. There was still a chance for him to save Rochelle.

"Come on, Jamie. Let's get in the car. We might be able to catch them. I'm not giving up yet."

They reached the car and jumped in.

Police sirens wailed in the distance and grew closer.

He got the car turned around and headed toward the street. He watched the van signal a right turn ahead.

The sirens grew louder. A police car pulled into the convenience store parking lot.

An officer got out and stalked toward their car. Matthew had no choice but to stop. He rolled down his window.

The officer leaned toward the open window. "We had a report of a woman being pushed into a van."

"Yes, it turned left about three blocks up." Matthew pointed. His hope renewed. Maybe the police would catch them.

"What color was the van?"

"White," said Matthew.

The officer rested his fingers on his police belt and shifted his weight. "Happen to catch any of the license plate?"

"No, but it's missing the side-view mirror on the passenger side. It fell off when I was hanging on to it."

"Give me a minute. There's another unit over in that direction." The officer ran back to his patrol car and radioed in the information.

Matthew got out of the car. "Officer, I know the woman who was kidnapped. Her name is Rochelle Miller."

The officer's expression changed. "Sir, I think you better come with me."

Matthew shook his head, not understanding. "I didn't have anything to do with her kidnapping. I tried to help her get away. Her son is with me."

"I know that. There's a Detective Bryan Keyes who I think you need to talk to."

* * *

From where she sat tied up in the back of the van, Rochelle couldn't see anything. The van swayed back and forth on the road and even slid several times, knocking her against the wall.

Finally it came to a stop. The side door opened, and one of the thugs came toward her holding another piece of fabric. She edged away from him but there was nowhere to go in the confined space. He tied the blindfold around her head. They were making sure she'd have no idea where she was.

A meaty, rough hand clutched her upper arm and yanked her out of the van. Her nerve endings seared from being jerked around and the sling for her injured arm had fallen off. She still had pain in her ribs from the accident. This level of brutality wasn't doing her any good.

Once outside the van, the thug pushed on her back. As she stepped forward, gravel crunched beneath her feet. A door squeaked as it swung open.

The man's voice pounded against her ear. "What are you waiting for? Get in there." She did as she was told. Her feet touched concrete. The air smelled like glue and oil.

The thug touched her back again. "You're about to go up some stairs."

At the top of the stairs, she stepped into a room that smelled musky. Again, the thug grabbed her upper arm and dragged her where he wanted her to go. His hands pressed on her shoulders. "Sit down."

She heard footsteps, a door closing and a key turning in a lock.

Her heart still hadn't stopped pounding. They hadn't

killed her outright. Maybe Elwood was still going to try to convince her to give up Jamie in exchange for her life. That was a lie, of course. He was going to kill her no matter what.

Elwood's head was so swollen with power he couldn't understand the strength of a mother's love.

She waited for what seemed like hours. The rope she'd been tied up with hadn't looked all that strong. She wiggled her hands back and forth, loosening it a little. The movement sent pain through her injured arm.

She heard a key turn in the lock. The door squeaked open and footsteps pounded across the floor.

She heard a man's heavy inhale and exhale of breath. He stepped in one direction and then in the other.

She turned her head toward the sound. Her heart fluttered as perspiration formed on her forehead. "Who's there?"

There was nothing but a long silence, though she could feel the heaviness of the man's presence in the room.

Finally, the man spoke up. "Megan, or should I say Rochelle, it's been such a long time since you and I had a chance to really talk."

"Elwood." The name tasted bitter on her tongue as every muscle in her body tensed.

Matthew held Jamie close when they got out of their car and stepped in behind the officer in the police station parking lot. He led them through a secure door and into a room with office carrels. They walked past a divider.

"Detective Keyes?" said the officer.

The man at the desk raised his head. Bryan Keyes

was about Matthew's age, with curly brown hair and a penetrating gaze.

The other officer stepped forward. "This is Matthew Stewart and Jamie, Rochelle Miller's son."

The detective pushed some papers on his desk to one side. "And where is Rochelle Miller?"

Still trying to sort through exactly what was going on, Matthew spoke up. "Some men took her in a van. I've no doubt they work for Elwood Corben."

The detective didn't seem perplexed by anything Matthew said.

"Why don't you two have a seat? Jamie, there's a couch over there you can sit on."

His shoulders drooping, Jamie trudged toward the couch. Matthew felt a knife go through his heart. Seeing Jamie fall apart like this was hard. He was a strong kid, but this could break the poor guy. Was there something more he could have done to get Rochelle out of that van?

Matthew walked over to Jamie and patted his back. "Can we get him some hot tea or cocoa or something? Maybe some food."

"No problem." Detective Bryan Keyes picked up the phone. "Hey, Bridget, I got a kid here who could use some food and something to drink."

Matthew took a seat closer to the detective's desk. He still wasn't quite sure what to think about Bryan Keyes. Was he in cahoots with Elwood or was there something else going on?

"So why didn't you meet us out at the picnic area?" Anger smoldered inside Matthew's gut. If this guy had only shown up, maybe Rochelle would be with him and Jamie right now.

"I got an urgent call on another case I'm working. I

had to go. The guy was scared. Said he had information I needed. Odd part was, when I got to the meeting place, there was nobody there."

Was Elwood involved in that? "Is it a case that's been in the newspapers?"

"Yes, and my name was mentioned as the lead detective on it." Detective Keyes sat back in his chair, maintaining eye contact with Matthew. He didn't seem defensive at all. None of his body language suggested he was lying or hiding anything.

The detective's excuse was starting to sound a little more viable. He had been played by Corben. "I guess that fits with what happened to us. We got ambushed by Elwood Corben and his buddies. Somehow Elwood found out about the meeting."

Detective Keyes looked directly at Matthew. "I'm sorry. You had no phone. There was no way to reach you."

"But how could Elwood know Rochelle called into the station?"

"We discovered my phone was bugged, along with several other officers'. We had some service work done a few days ago. That must have been when they were put in."

The detective leaned forward. "I was willing to take Rochelle's story, but I was a little pessimistic since you called in those two false alarms. You guys had kind of been blacklisted. When all this other stuff went down, I knew something was up and that you were probably telling the truth. So I started doing a little digging."

Matthew shifted in his chair. He found himself feeling more hopeful than he had in a long time. Maybe the police would help them now. "Did you find evidence of Dylan Corben's murder?"

"Not quite. But we get notifications anytime a body is found anywhere in the Northwest, in case we can match it to a missing person or cold case that we have on file."

A female officer came in with tray full of food for Jamie. The boy said thank-you and dove into his sandwich like a hungry tiger.

Matthew scooted his chair a little closer to Bryan's desk. "So what did you find?"

"It seems an unidentified body surfaced in the Seattle area in an abandoned warehouse. Judging from the degree of decomp they estimate it to be about eight to ten years old." Bryan swung around in his chair.

"And you think that body might be Dylan?"

"It's a possibility. What day did Elwood Corben show up here?"

"That would have been the day of Rochelle's accident. The tenth." That seemed like a thousand years ago. He glanced over at Jamie, who was chugging down his carton of milk.

Bryan clicked through a couple of screens on his computer. "The body was discovered about a week before that."

"That would allow for the time it took Elwood to find Rochelle," Matthew said.

The female officer angled her body around the divider. "Bryan, you asked to be kept updated about finding that van."

"Yes."

Matthew's ears perked up.

"The officer doing the pursuit lost them, but he can

provide a general direction they were heading," said the female officer.

Matthew's optimism deflated. None of this new information made a bit of difference if they couldn't get to Rochelle in time. Or worse, if she was already dead.

THIRTEEN

Rochelle wasn't sure if she was shivering because the room was cold or because Elwood was in it. His voice cut through to the bone. Her skin crawled with every word he said.

"Now, Rochelle, my dear. I would like to get a few things straightened out with you and then maybe both of us can be on our way."

She doubted that was true. "You killed Dylan. You killed the man I loved." The rage rose up inside her. For ten years she had pushed it down, but now that the reason for her anger was out in the open, it threatened to explode.

Elwood laughed. "Dylan is not dead."

All her racing thoughts halted. What was he talking about?

"I saw him die." Elwood's words caused a tiny bud of hope to blossom inside. Was it possible that Jamie's father was alive?

"What happened at the house was an unfortunate accident. I lost my temper and for that I am deeply regretful. If you had stayed around long enough instead of running like a scared rabbit, you would have known. I called an ambulance. He was fine."

Rochelle struggled to sort through what Elwood was telling her. "But why have you been trying to hurt me?"

"You never gave me time to explain." Elwood's footsteps pounded on the floor.

The news that Dylan might be alive overshadowed her memories of what happened the night she ran away from Seattle. "You threatened me and my family."

"Poor Dylan was so heartbroken about you running, he wanted to leave the country. I set him up in one of our foreign offices." Elwood sounded sure of himself, almost cocky.

Her throat constricted. Her whole world was being turned upside down. "That's not true. I saw him on the floor. I saw the blood. He wasn't moving." She struggled to make this information fit what she had observed. Even then, she wondered if her memories were distorted by the trauma of the event.

"Are you sure your memory is clear on that?" Elwood continued to pace. "You were distraught and so young and, as it turns out, pregnant with my grandson."

Everything had happened so fast that night. Had she merely filled in the blanks with what she thought she saw? She shook her head. "Prove it to me. Show me that Dylan is still alive."

Elwood's footsteps grew louder. His rough hands touched her face and she jerked away.

"Hold still, I'm trying to take the blindfold off." Elwood voice revealed the barely contained rage that she remembered. No one defied him. No one dared disagree with him.

She allowed him to remove the blindfold. She caught the acrid scent of his cologne as he leaned close and lifted the fabric from her face. He stepped back. She looked into his narrow, bloodshot eyes but couldn't discern anything from his neutral expression. Elwood was a practiced liar.

His head cocked to one side, and the corner of his mouth turned up. "I will say my son has good taste in women."

Rochelle took in her surroundings. The place was filled with debris, papers and cardboard and soda and beer cans. The knocked-over file cabinet in the corner with open drawers and the three-legged desk indicated that this had been an office at one time.

Elwood held a phone in his hand. He clicked through several buttons. "This is a photo he sent me several months ago from our Hong Kong office."

He angled the phone so Rochelle could see. Her breath caught. The photo did look like an older Dylan, same intense gaze, same wavy hair. He was standing on a city street, neon flashing behind him. His bright smile seemed to illuminate the photograph.

She still wasn't convinced. Photos could be doctored. She couldn't help herself. Despite her pessimism, the thought of seeing Dylan again, of Jamie having a father, caused the hope to grow inside her. Was it possible? Dylan would get to see his son. "Did he ever get married?" She braced for the answer.

"No, over the years there have been a few women, but he didn't seem to want to commit to them. I don't think he ever got over you."

"I want to talk to him," Rochelle said.

"I thought you would say that." He narrowed his eyes. "I just wonder what I get out of the deal after my character has been maligned by the lies you told the local police about me."

Rochelle shook her head. "I don't know what you're talking about."

He narrowed his eyes at her. "You told them I was a murderer."

"I just want to hear Dylan's voice," she pleaded.

He smashed his fist against his open palm. "And I want to see my grandson that you have kept from me. That's the deal I'd like to make with you."

So that was his game. "If Dylan is alive and well why didn't you just come to me and tell me? Why go to all this trouble and violence?" Her voice took on a desperate quality as she struggled to discern the truth. "Why didn't you just tell Dylan you found me? He could have gotten in touch me. And why didn't you come here sooner? Why did you wait ten years?" She squeezed her eyes shut to keep the tears from coming.

She was surprised at all the emotion, the hope and the confusion that welled up to the surface. There were holes in Elwood's story. She knew that. But her desire for Jamie to have a father was still so strong it didn't take much to get her head all twisted around.

Elwood stopped pacing. He sat down on the file cabinet and crossed his arms. Elwood knew how to play people. He was saying what she wanted to hear.

Her resolve solidified inside her. "I will not let you near Jamie, no matter what. If Dylan is alive, I can find some other way to get in touch with him." Even as she uttered the words, she knew they weren't true. If she didn't agree to give Elwood what he wanted, she had no chance at all of getting out of here alive. But no matter what happened to her, she had to protect Jamie at all costs.

Elwood exploded across the floor and rammed his face close to hers. "I just want to see my grandson." He punched every word as he spit them out.

She jerked her head back. His breath smelled sour. She studied him for a moment. His gaze pierced through her. She did not believe for a moment that Elwood Corben only wanted to *see* his grandson. Elwood's relationships had always been about possessing and controlling, not about being reasonable or loving.

He turned his back to her. After a long moment, he swung back around, his face like a mask, revealing nothing.

"Well, my dear." He stalked toward her and pulled the blindfold back over her face, patting her cheek when he was done. "I'll give you a little time to think about my offer."

His footsteps pounded across the floor, and she heard the door ease open and then shut. The lock clicked back into place.

Rochelle slumped forward. She felt as though she'd been punched in the stomach. Elwood had twisted her mind into so many knots she couldn't think straight. Chances were he was lying to get what he wanted. But still, she could not let go of the hope that Dylan might be alive. Was it possible?

She couldn't think about that now. She needed to get out of here before he came back. It was the only chance she had of staying alive and getting back to Jamie. She tried to remember the layout of the room from the few minutes she'd had to take in her surroundings.

She struggled to loosen the rope that bound her

hands, but twisting her hands only caused the rope to dig into her wrists. She rose to her feet and leaned over so her face was close to the back of the chair while she tried to hook the blindfold on the top part of the chair and then ease her way down to the floor. She managed to move the fabric high enough on her forehead so that when she tilted her head back, she could see.

She walked around the room looking for something, anything that might help her cut the rope around her wrists. She spotted a piece of glass by the three-legged desk. She slipped down to the floor and backed up to the vicinity of the glass, patting the dusty floor with her hands until she found it. She worked the glass back and forth over the rope until she felt it loosening. The glass sliced her skin and she winced but kept sliding it across the rope.

Once her hands were free, she pulled the blindfold off. The pain had returned to her injured arm. She jumped to her feet and dashed toward the door. She wiggled the knob, but it was locked. Frustrated and desperate, she wanted to shake the door as hard as she could, but chances were Elwood had left a guard around if he wasn't still outside himself. She didn't want to alert him to the fact that she was no longer tied up.

She paced the floor. There had to be another way out of there. She saw a small, dusty window beside the door. She used the fabric from the blindfold to clear the window. She was on the second floor of some sort of abandoned manufacturing facility. The building had a high ceiling. She could see the walkway and the stairs that led up to the office. Down below, she could see one man in a hoodie and ski jacket walking back and forth. He didn't look like any of the other thugs she'd seen before. The man stopped to adjust his ear bud and then pulled an iPod out of his pocket. How fortunate. He probably wouldn't hear any noise she made.

Once the thug turned his back, Rochelle grabbed the chair and slammed it through the window. She grabbed the broken leg from the three-legged desk to break out the rest of the glass. She placed the chair beneath the window and peered out.

The man down below continued to walk back and forth with his head down. Aware that her movement might catch the attention of her guard, she slipped through the window as quickly as possible. She reached her hands out for the landing outside the office, putting most her weight on her good arm. As she pulled her feet through the window and crouched, a sharp pain shot through her rib cage, reminding her that she still was not totally healed from the accidents.

Rochelle surveyed her surroundings. There was only one way down and one way out. Even a guard who was not dedicated to his job would see her. As she stared at the high ceiling, she wondered if all her effort had been for nothing.

From the couch where he sat by a sleeping Jamie, Matthew watched as Bryan Keyes returned to his desk from another part of the station.

Bryan said, "We may have located Rochelle. We think that she may have been taken to an area on the north side with some abandoned buildings. Not much activity down that way. We've got unmarked units searching every building now."

Matthew felt helpless. He wanted to be out there looking for her. Jamie stirred in his sleep. The boy rested his head on Matthew's leg. As frustrated as he felt, he knew that the best place for him to be was watching over Jamie. If…no…when they found Rochelle, he knew it would ease her mind to know that Jamie had been taken care of. "I hope they find her and catch Elwood."

"I tell you one thing. Elwood Corben is not leaving the city by car for at least two days. No one is. Those passes are snowed over. Meantime, we have officers watching the airport." Bryan slammed a file folder down on his desk. "You're free to go. We can keep you updated on the progress if you give us a phone number."

Matthew touched the pocket where he usually kept his cell phone. "I lost my phone. Guess I'm going to have to pick one up somewhere."

Matthew thought about what he might do. Was it safe for him to go back to his house? Certainly he couldn't risk taking Jamie there. "I'll call you with the number as soon as I get a phone." He rose to his feet and turned to face Bryan. "This Elwood Corben guy, he's after the kid, too."

"We can have a patrol car follow you home," Bryan said.

"I don't think I should go home, not with Jamie, but I do know where I can take him. Rochelle had mentioned a place she'd stayed when she was pregnant with Jamie. I'm going to take him to Naomi's Place."

Bryan lifted his fingers off the keyboard and turned to Matthew. "I know that place. It's a long story. Years ago, the woman who is now my fiancée stayed there." His gaze darkened. "The baby she gave up for adoption was ours. We got together ten years later."

Matthew detected a level of intense emotion in Bryan's voice. "I'm glad things worked out for the two of you."

"Sarah, my fiancée, knew a woman named Rochelle when she was there. I just didn't realize it was the same Rochelle on this police report." Bryan rose to his feet. "Let me get a patrol officer to follow you out there." He cupped Matthew's shoulder. "I'm going to do everything I can to get her back safe."

Matthew offered him his hand to shake. "We both will." The ache in his gut that had started when he saw Rochelle being driven away in the van had not subsided. But he had to hope she was still okay. For Jamie's sake, he couldn't give up.

He lifted the sleeping Jamie up from the couch. The boy's glasses were askew on his face, and his cheeks were rosy. Jamie barely stirred as Matthew carried him out to Daniel's car, placed him in the passenger seat and belted him in.

As Matthew drove, the patrol car followed about two car lengths behind them. After he keyed in the address on Daniel's navigation system, he stopped at a store to pick up a cell phone. Then he called Naomi's Place. He was a stranger showing up at their door. He thought it better to call first and let them know the situation. They might not even be open to him showing up with Jamie.

A young-sounding woman answered the phone. "Hello, Naomi's Place."

Matthew explained his situation, telling the woman that Jamie was the child of a woman who had lived there ten years ago. "It's a long story, but the kid needs a safe place to stay."

"I'm not sure what we do in a situation like this." The woman on the other end of the line paused for a moment. "Probably you should come over and talk directly to Naomi. I'll tell her you're on your way."

Matthew said thank you and hung up.

Naomi's Place was a converted schoolhouse with a small sign out front. They found parking in the back. As he got out of the car, he waved at the police officer in the patrol car. "I think we'll be okay."

Jamie was awake though he was still blinking rapidly. He straightened his glasses. "Did they find my mom yet?"

Matthew felt that familiar stab to his heart. "We're working on it, buddy." What he wouldn't give for Jamie never to have pain in his life. He felt protective of the kid. This was more than any child should endure.

"What is this place?" Jamie stared through the windshield.

"Well, believe it or not, when your mom was about to have you, she stayed here."

Jamie let out a breath and sort of half smiled. "Naomi's Place. Mom told me about it. She said it was the most special place in the world. She helps with a fundraiser every year, but I've never been here." He looked at the building as though they'd just driven up to an amusement park.

"Let's go inside." Matthew waited for Jamie to join him on the steps. He draped an arm over the boy and leaned forward to knock on the door.

He heard footsteps, and the door swung open. A woman who was probably in her forties and wearing an apron smiled down at them. "Yes?"

"This might sound a little crazy to you, but I'm a

friend of Rochelle Miller's. She stayed here years ago when she had Jamie." He touched the top of the boy's head. "We talked to a young woman on the phone just a few minutes ago."

Recognition spread across the woman's face. "Oh, my Jamie. I held you when you were just a tiny baby. My name is Claire. I've been the cook here for over fifteen years."

"We're in a bit of a dilemma. The young woman I talked to said I should speak directly to Naomi," Matthew said.

"I'll go get Naomi then. Why don't the two of you come in?" She stepped back so they could enter. "There's a lounge just around the corner."

Claire led them down a hallway and into a large room filled with a hodgepodge of couches, chairs and love seats. A teenage girl sat at a piano in the far corner playing a soft tune. "Make yourself at home. I think Naomi is upstairs doing Bible study with some of the girls. I'll let her know. She'll come down in a little bit. In the meantime, are the two of you hungry?"

Jamie rubbed his stomach. "Yeah."

Matthew smiled. Jamie had just had food at the station. For such a skinny kid, he sure consumed the calories.

Claire laughed. "We have ham-and-Swiss sandwiches. I'll see to it that you get some."

As Jamie wandered around, Matthew sat down to watch the young girl playing piano. Her long, slim fingers moved delicately up and down the keyboard. She smiled at Jamie when he stopped to listen to her play.

Being in this place only made him admire Rochelle more. She'd come here scared and alone. Because of

Elwood, she had even deeper reasons to be afraid besides facing having a child by herself.

Jamie sat beside the girl at the piano, and she started to play "Chopsticks." A tall woman with black hair streaked with silver came into the room. She held out a hand as Matthew stood up. "I'm Naomi, the director here. I understand you are a friend of Rochelle Miller's. I got the phone message from Angie."

He shook her hand.

She glanced over toward the piano, her voice filling with affection. "And this, I know, is Jamie. Rochelle has brought him to the fund-raiser we hold at the Holiday Inn ballroom a few times, and I get a picture every Christmas."

"Yeah, he's a pretty good guy," Matthew said.

"I can see you care a great deal about him," Naomi said.

"Sorry if this is an inconvenience. This is the only safe place for Jamie to be right now," Matthew said. "Rochelle was a witness to a crime ten years ago. I'm afraid it has caught up with her. A man wants her dead and he wants Jamie."

"That serious?" Once the shock faded from her expression, Naomi studied Matthew for a minute. "You know that winter when she was here waiting for Jamie to be born, it seemed she was afraid of something more than just being a single mom. Jamie is welcome to stay here. I can't allow you to stay overnight, though."

"I understand. Hopefully this will be resolved quickly." Very quickly, if Rochelle was already dead. He shut down that thought as rapidly as it had come into his head. He had to stay optimistic.

"Rochelle is fortunate to have a boyfriend like you. I was wondering if she would ever meet someone."

"Oh, I'm just a friend," Matthew said.

Naomi hesitated before answering as her gaze returned to Jamie. "You certainly have taken on a great deal for just being a friend."

Something about the openness of Naomi's expression made it easy for him to talk to her. "I guess somewhere along the line I started hoping there might be more than a friendship." It had been a thought that had played at the corners of his mind for a long time. When he said it out loud, he knew it was true.

"It takes longer for someone like Rochelle to trust because of all she has been through," Naomi said.

Naomi was probably right, but time was something they didn't have.

When the girl at the piano left the room, Jamie wandered around looking at the photographs on the wall. He pointed to one. "That's my mom."

Naomi and Matthew walked over to him.

Naomi placed a hand on Jamie's shoulder. "Oh, yes, that was the Christmas that your mother was here. Those were her two best friends, Clarissa—" Naomi pointed to a petite blond woman in the picture and then at a woman with long brown hair "—and Sarah."

"Yeah, I met Sarah's fiancé. He's a police officer," Matthew said.

"Their story had a happy ending." Naomi pointed again to Clarissa. "And I was able to get back in touch with Clarissa after ten years. I'm planning a reunion for the women who were here ten years ago. Maybe Rochelle will be able to come."

"I don't know about that." He didn't know what

was going to happen in the next hour let alone the next month. He didn't know if Rochelle was dead or alive.

Naomi studied him for a long moment. "I understand, but I will pray that I'll see both of you there and maybe even Jamie."

His phone rang. It was Bryan Keyes's cell number. "I have to take this."

Naomi nodded and directed Jamie away so Matthew could have some privacy.

Matthew clicked on his phone.

"Just wanted to let you know. The white van was spotted off Evens Street by the old car upholstery place. We're closing in. Hopefully, we'll have some good news for you in a little while."

"Thanks for filling me in. I'll keep the phone close." As Matthew ended the call, he felt his frustration rising. He couldn't just wait here and hope for a good outcome. He wanted to know that he had done everything he could to save Rochelle's life. Even though he knew the police would do their job, he had to go out to where they thought Rochelle was.

He walked over to Naomi and Jamie. "If it's all right with Naomi, I need to go help your mom," he told the boy. "Do you mind staying here for a while?"

"Not if it means I get to see my mom again," Jamie said. "Besides, I like it here."

Naomi touched his shoulder. "You do what you have to do. We'll look out for Jamie."

Matthew raced out of the room and down the hallway. He jumped in Daniel's car and pulled out of the parking lot. His heart was pounding by the time he turned out onto the street.

Bryan hadn't said anything about spotting Elwood

Corben. Maybe they wouldn't catch him today, but they would take him down in time. All he wanted right now was to see Rochelle safe again…and maybe hold her in his arms.

FOURTEEN

Rochelle waited until the guard had his back turned to dart down the stairs a few at a time. She prayed that the man would not notice the broken window. If he did, she had nowhere to hide. She peered above the solid railing. The guard had wandered to the threshold where a large door was missing. He stared outside with his back to Rochelle. She ran down the remaining stairs and searched for a hiding place on the ground floor.

When the guard stepped outside, she could see that a dark SUV had pulled up. She dashed behind a ratty-looking pile of car seats that were stripped down to the springs.

"Go get her now." The panic-filled voice was Elwood's. "We just spotted a police car."

She had seconds to get outside before they realized she'd escaped. She heard footsteps pound on the concrete.

"What is going on here?" Elwood shouted as both men ran up the stairs.

Elwood's shouts and curses hit her ears as she raced toward the door.

"There she is," shouted the guard.

The sunlight nearly blinded her when she stepped outside. She looked one way and then the other, not recognizing any landmarks. She raced toward Elwood's SUV and yanked open the door. No chance of escape there. He'd taken the keys out of the ignition.

The two men burst outside. Elwood shouted something at the guard, who sprinted in her direction.

She ran toward another building. Of course Elwood wouldn't do the chasing. If the police were in the area, he probably wanted to leave as quickly as possible.

Her boots sank into the deep snow as she ran around the building. The guard was closing the distance between them. She willed herself to move faster despite her freezing feet and legs. All she had to do was hold out until the police got here.

She was out of breath as she came to an unplowed street. Still no sign of a police car. The snow was almost too deep to navigate through. The guard was about ten paces behind her, but moving just as slowly as she was in the deep snow. Her heart pounded against her rib cage as she struggled to take in a breath.

She needed to get to a plowed street or find a place to hide. The guard reached out for her, grabbing the hem of her coat. She turned and scratched his face. He let go, and she trudged forward sinking down in the snow with each step. The man still pursued her but with much less enthusiasm.

See, Elwood, that's what you get when you hire other people to do your dirty work.

She backed around the other side of building. When she looked over her shoulder, she could no longer see the guard. She came out on a plowed street but stopped short when she saw Elwood's SUV parked half a block away with the motor running. She took off sprinting in the opposite direction. Elwood rolled the car toward her, gaining speed. She ran faster. She'd get bogged down in the drifts if she tried to escape off the road, but Elwood wouldn't be able to follow her in his car.

When Elwood's car was within feet of her, he revved the engine, and she made her move. She jumped off the road. Her boot sank down into the snow, but she pulled her foot free of the snow as it suctioned around her leg. She took a laborious step and then another. The only sign of shelter she saw was a grain elevator some forty yards away.

Elwood had stopped his car and gotten out. He leaned on the hood, a pistol in his hand. Rochelle felt as though the world moved in slow motion as she watched him raise and aim the pistol. Had he given up on trying to use her to get to Jamie or did he only intend to wound her?

She froze for a moment like a deer in the headlights. A body came at her from the side and knocked her to the ground just as the shot shattered the winter silence. For a moment, she was completely surrounded by snow. Cold water dripped down her cheeks and weighed down her eyelashes. She looked to see who had knocked her over. Matthew shouted into her face and it took her a moment to realize what he was saying. "Don't run in a straight line."

He grabbed her hand and pulled her to her feet. In a zigzag pattern, he made his way toward a place where the snow had drifted away and was less deep. Elwood shot one more time before getting in his car and rolling along the road, probably hoping to line up another shot.

They were in deep snow again. Their only option was to crouch down if he chose to shoot again.

They were ten yards from the grain silos when Elwood's guard circled around the cylindrical metal structure. He landed a blow to Matthew's jaw. Droplets of blood spread across the white snow, and Matthew bent forward.

The guard yanked Rochelle's uninjured arm at the elbow. "You're coming with me."

Rochelle beat on his hand where he held her, but his grip was like iron. Matthew raised his head, still clutching his jaw. His mouth and nose were bleeding. He stumbled toward them as the guard dragged her through the snow.

Elwood waited in the SUV on the road, his engine running.

Matthew landed a blow to the back of the man's head and both of them fell into the snow, rolling around and throwing punches.

Elwood had gotten out of his car and was stalking toward them.

Rochelle dove in, trying to pull the guard off Matthew as they fought. She hooked her arm around his neck and pulled. The guard turned his rage on her, elbowing her in the stomach.

Elwood drew closer. He still held the gun.

With the wind knocked out of her from the blow, Rochelle fell backward in the snow. She stared at the sky, unable to breathe for a moment. Matthew jumped on top of the guard, landing a blow to his solar plexus. Matthew backed away as the guard turned sideways in the snow and retched.

Rochelle wheezed in air. Matthew grabbed her hand

and pulled her to her feet. Elwood was midway between the road and them when they heard the sirens. He pivoted and raced back to his car, jumping in and driving away. He turned up a plowed street and disappeared.

The police car came from the opposite direction about a minute later. It stopped, and an officer got out.

Matthew ran over to meet him, and Rochelle followed him. He pointed to the guard, who was still lying in the snow. "That man attacked us. Elwood Corben just went that way."

"I'll radio it in," said the officer. "There's another unit nearby."

Rochelle pressed close to Matthew. "What's going on? Why are the police helping us now?"

Matthew turned to face her. "Boy, do I have a lot to tell you."

Matthew watched as the officer took Elwood's guard into custody. He wiped the blood from his face with his sleeve and then bent over gripping his knees and trying to catch his breath.

Once the thug was in the backseat, the officer turned toward them. "Do you two need a ride back into town?"

Matthew shook his head and edged closer to Rochelle. "My car is just a few blocks over. I got this."

The police officer got into his car and pulled away.

"I wonder if they will get Elwood." Rochelle looked weary.

"I hope so." They trudged through the snow back to Daniel's car. He opened the passenger-side door for her.

She didn't get in but stopped by the door to ask, "Is Jamie okay?"

"Yes, he's safe at Naomi's Place." Her face was still

etched with concern. He'd do anything to ease her worry. "He feels very comfortable there. Naomi made him feel right at home."

"Thank you for taking care of him and for coming for me." An affectionate brightness flashed through her eyes.

Even though there was a car door between them, he reached up and touched her cheek. "I had to take care of the two of you."

Still looking into his eyes, she tilted her head. "No, you've gone way beyond your job description for us. I think this stopped being about my recovery and Jamie still having a mom a while ago." She reached up and touched his cheek. "You have blood from where that guy hit you." She pulled off her glove and stroked his cheek with her finger. Her touch was as delicate as silk.

He locked into her gaze, feeling the magnetic pull of it. He leaned closer to her and kissed her, just the brush of a feather across her mouth. Her eyes grew wide as he pulled back. She touched her hand to his cheek but then looked away.

The inner glow from the kiss lingered. "Get in the car. I have a lot to tell you."

Rochelle slipped in and buckled her seat belt. As he started the engine, he could feel the weight of her gaze on him. Was she thinking about the kiss, too?

He cleared his throat. "First of all, Bryan Keyes is a good guy. You weren't wrong about him."

"Good to know my character meter isn't broken." Her voice still had that smoldering quality.

"Officer Keyes thinks he might have found the reason Elwood came for you after all this time. It seems an unidentified body was found in Seattle, and it's believed to be ten years old," Matthew said.

Rochelle was silent for a moment. She glanced out the window and then back at him. The mood in the car shifted. "So for sure, Jamie was okay with staying at Naomi's Place?"

She seemed distracted, not able to absorb the news.

"Is there something going on? I thought you'd be elated to know the reason Elwood came back."

She shook her head and then played with the zipper of her ski jacket. "Elwood led me to believe that Dylan was still alive. I guess I wanted to believe it."

"And if he was alive?"

She shook her head. "I don't know. When Elwood said that, I just thought if it were true, maybe we could be a real family like it should have been all along."

Matthew wrestled with disappointment. He understood the connection she had to the father of her child, but somehow it made the kiss between them seem less meaningful. If Dylan was alive, would she go back to him for Jamie's sake? "They haven't identified the body yet." Matthew tried to keep the hurt out of his voice. "Officer Keyes seems to think it makes sense that the body would be Dylan's, the timing of everything."

His car slid a little bit on the road. Up ahead, a snowplow moved toward them on the opposite side of the road.

"I think I want to go see Jamie first thing before I talk to Officer Keyes," Rochelle said.

She seemed to be closing down. He wondered if the kiss had meant anything to her. He peered through the windshield. The snowplow had drifted into their lane.

Rochelle gripped the armrest. "What is that guy doing?"

Matthew slowed down. The plow driver still had not corrected.

"He's coming straight at us," Rochelle shrieked.

Matthew stopped and shifted into Reverse, but the plow loomed toward them. It dropped its bucket, making a screeching noise as it scraped the road. Matthew pressed the accelerator as the plow closed the distance between them. When he reached a side street he attempted to swing into it backward so he could get turned around, but it was too late. The plow collided with their car and pushed it into a snowbank.

Rochelle screamed as the car tilted on its side. He reached out for her, grasping her hand. The noise of crunching metal surrounded them.

"I've got you, Rochelle." He squeezed her hand. The view through his window was nothing but snow.

"Are they going to crush us?"

The pressure on the car subsided. The plow backed up, though their car was still at an angle and stuck in a snowbank. The oppressive clanging of the snowplow's engine stopped.

Rochelle's door creaked open. She screamed as two large hands reached in and cut the seat belt. Down below her, Matthew unclicked his own seat belt. He grabbed her hand as the man above her tried to pull her out.

"Let go of her." He wrapped his arms around her waist as she was lifted up. He saw daylight just as a boot slammed into his face. His eyes stung from the blow, and he fell back down to the bottom of the car. Above him he could hear Rochelle screaming and kicking. He stood up and prepared to crawl out.

"Should we waste that guy?" the thug said.

"No, find out what the boss wants," said another.

A face peered down through the open door. Scarface. "Get out of there."

What choice did he have? There was no other way out. He crawled to the surface. Rochelle had already been dragged down the snow pile. He watched them lead her toward a car parked behind the plow, right before a hood went over his head. He yanked the hood off, turned around and slammed his fist into Scarface's jaw.

The thug lost his balance and rolled down the snow pile. Matthew dove down toward him, prepared to take him on, but the second thug came back holding a gun with one hand. His other hand was clamped around Rochelle's forearm.

"Knock it off. Or I'll just waste you right here," he snarled.

The other thug pushed Matthew from behind. "Get in the car." He bound Matthew's hands in front of him and then slipped a hood over his head again right before he shoved him in the backseat.

Matthew pressed close to Rochelle, touching his bound hands to her knee, hoping to provide her with some reassurance. Why he thought that was a good idea he didn't know. Why was he offering her hope in a situation that now seemed hopeless?

He could feel the car rolling along the road and turning. He counted the turns and estimated how long they'd been traveling. All the windows were rolled up so he couldn't hear or smell anything that would indicate where they were going. He guessed that they had traveled at least half an hour. Since the interstates were closed, they must be on one of the country roads that led out of town.

Finally, the car rolled to a stop, and they both were yanked from the backseat. He could feel packed snow beneath his feet as the thugs prodded them to move. A door opened, and they were pushed inside. The room smelled of cleaning products, and he could hear a fire crackling. He sensed, too, that someone else was in the room besides the two thugs.

"Take their hoods off." The voice held a sinister tone. Though he'd never heard the man speak, he was pretty sure it was Elwood. "Search them for cell phones."

After removing the hoods, Scarface patted Matthew down while the other searched Rochelle. Matthew caught the desperate pleading in Rochelle's eyes. The thug tossed Matthew's new cell phone over to Elwood.

"Please, have a seat," said Elwood with feigned politeness.

As he and Rochelle settled onto a couch opposite Elwood, Matthew glanced around. They were in a log cabin. All the curtains were pulled on the windows, so he couldn't see outside. He had no idea if they were out in the middle of nowhere or close to civilization. Elwood had probably rented the place. It wasn't a cabin he recognized. A rustic pine coffee table lay between Elwood and them. What looked like photographs turned facedown were spread across the table.

Elwood bent his head sideways and stared at Rochelle with narrow, snakelike eyes. "So good to see the two of you again."

Rochelle scooted closer to Matthew. She glanced around the cabin, as well.

"So I thought I'd give you one more chance. I'd like

to see my grandson." Barely contained rage colored his words. "And don't say *over my dead body* because I can arrange that, Rochelle."

His words cut sharper than a knife. Matthew saw murder in his eyes.

"You have no right to see Jamie." Rochelle's voice held unexpected strength.

Elwood cocked an eyebrow at her. "So you say." He held Matthew's phone up. "Do you think that I can't find him on my own?" His lips curled back from his teeth and he raised his voice. "I was doing you a favor."

He clicked through Matthew's phone. "Mr. Stewart, this looks like a very new phone. I see you have made exactly two phone calls. And one is a number I recognize." He looked at Rochelle. "How do you think I figured out who your friends were?"

Rochelle shook her head as her eyes grew wide with fear.

He flipped over the photographs one by one. Pictures of Rochelle and Jamie with different people. Rochelle had written names and dates on the border of the photos. "We went through your house. We found your purse at work with the phone. Jamie isn't with any of your friends. You were at least that smart."

He turned the final photograph over, a picture of Rochelle in evening dress at a fund-raiser. "It was a long shot, but it seems that you have some sort of connection to this Naomi's Place. We looked up the number. It's the same number that Matthew called earlier today."

Rochelle jerked slightly but, to her credit, her face remained neutral. Only the way she tightly laced her fingers together gave away how shocked she was.

Matthew clenched his jaw. Elwood had figured out where Jamie was.

"You don't know anything." She held her voice steady, but her fingers had turned white from how firmly she squeezed them together.

"I have no more need for either of you." Elwood looked at one of the thugs standing at the back of the room. "Take them outside and deal with them. Far enough away so their bodies won't be found until spring, preferably never."

One of the thugs grabbed Matthew's shirt collar from the back and yanked him up. "Let's get out of here."

Matthew felt a rage like he had never known before. Elwood Corben was pure evil; at the very least he was a sociopath. He turned suddenly and lunged at him. He knocked Elwood to the floor and smacked him in the face with his bound hands before the thugs pulled him off. He dove again for Elwood as the older man tried to get to his feet.

"Hey, the girl," one of the thugs shouted.

The door was wide-open and Rochelle was gone.

FIFTEEN

Rochelle burst out into the dark night. The cabin and the vehicles parked by it were the only thing she saw besides forest. They were out in the middle of nowhere. She heard the shouting from inside the cabin. Hindered by her bound hands, Rochelle ran toward the trees. The yelling behind her grew more intense as the men came outside. She picked up on the tone of confusion in their words. They hadn't figured out which way she'd gone.

As she worked her way through the evergreens, she struggled to come up with a plan that made sense. She needed to double back, help Matthew escape and get a car. Had they simply shot him first or put their energy into finding her? She calmed her fears by telling herself she hadn't heard gunshots.

Then her pulse raced as thoughts about Jamie bombarded her, and she nearly doubled over from the terror of what might happen to him. She pushed herself a little farther into the forest and slipped behind a tree to catch her breath.

At one point, it sounded like one of the men may have ventured into the trees, judging from how loud his voice became.

She couldn't wait here forever. She had to go help Matthew and then they needed to find a way to warn Naomi.

She pushed away from the tree trunk and stepped carefully back toward the cabin. When she peered around a corner of the cabin, one of the cars was pulling out. She slipped back into the shadows the eaves provided, fearing the headlights of the turning car would give her away. She angled her head so she had a view of the front yard again. This time, she saw the red glare of taillights as the car pulled out onto the road, leaving two trucks parked in front of the cabin. She'd seen two people in the car. They must be heading into town to get Jamie. The prospect of them finding Jamie nearly paralyzed her with fear.

Rochelle worked her way around the cabin until she found a window. Through a small opening between the curtains, she had a view of Matthew's legs where he sat on the couch, and also the thug, Scarface, who sat opposite him holding a gun and resting it on his thigh while he stared at Matthew. The thug ran his finger up and down the barrel of the gun.

So this guy had been left behind to finish off Matthew and probably look for her in the woods. If she had to venture a guess based on his body language, she'd say the thug was having some hesitation about killing Matthew.

She circled back around to the front of the cabin. When she tried the door, it opened. A narrow foyer provided some cover for her. She could only guess at how much time she had before the thug worked up the courage to do what he'd been ordered to do.

"I don't want to kill you. I never wanted to kill anyone," said Scarface. He laid the gun on the table.

"So don't kill me. Just let me go. Say I escaped."

The thug was slow in responding. "Elwood would figure it out. You don't understand. He's got me over a barrel. I owe him money, big-time. This is how I repay the debt." There was tone of distress in Scarface's voice. "Elwood never said I'd have to kill someone. That guy is crazy obsessive."

"There has to be another way," Matthew said.

"There is no other way. If I don't kill you, Elwood will kill me." After a long silence, the thug said. "Get up on your feet and turn your back to me."

The words chilled Rochelle to the core. She took in a sharp breath. She had to act now. When she angled around the wall of the foyer, Scarface had his back to her and was reaching for the gun.

She scanned her surroundings, looking for something to use as a weapon. She picked up a lamp, but with her hands tied together her range of motion was limited. The thug heard her and turned just as she hit him on the head. The blow stunned him but didn't knock him down. The gun went flying. Matthew took advantage of Scarface's momentary disability to kick the back of the thug's knees, causing him to crumple to the ground.

"Hurry." They ran outside toward the truck. Matthew swung open the driver's-side door. "There's a knife in my coat pocket. You need to cut me free."

With a frantic glance toward the open door of the cabin, she dug into his pocket, retrieved the knife and cut him free.

"Now hold on to the knife and cut yourself free," he said.

Rochelle jumped in and sliced through her restraints. She pointed to the empty ignition switch. "No keys. Another chance to use your misspent youth, huh?"

He pulled the sun visor down and felt along it, then held out a key. "Sometimes you get lucky." He started up the engine just as Scarface appeared in the doorway.

Matthew hit the gas and spun around to face the road. Though the road was still snow packed, he sped up.

"We have to get to a phone and warn Naomi." Rochelle's stomach tightened into a knot. If she thought too much about what might happen to Jamie and the others, she'd shut down.

Matthew leaned forward and peered out the windshield. "There has to be something up this way. A gas station or something."

She stared out at the dark landscape. "This is the road we were on when that blond guy took me from the hospital." That seemed like a thousand years ago.

Matthew glanced out the side window. "Yeah, it does look like it." He shook his head. "I never even arranged to have my car towed."

Matthew's life had been turned upside down by meeting her. He'd given up so much. "It's not like you've had time."

"Being around you is certainly not boring." He gave her a quick smile and then turned his attention back to the road.

Matthew could have been bitter or upset about how his life had been disrupted. But it wasn't in his nature to respond to situations that way.

"Matthew, you've done so much for me and for Jamie. I don't understand why."

"At first it was because I wanted to make sure you

were okay physically. I didn't listen to my instinct on another call we had a while ago, and I wasn't going to do that again."

"At first?"

"Then I guess I didn't back out because I didn't want Jamie to lose his mother." His voice became choked up. "I don't know what I would do if something happened to that kid."

Rochelle sat back in her seat with her eyes still on Matthew. "No one's ever cared that much about my son besides me."

"He's a good kid. No, he's…he's a great kid." His voice faltered. He took in a breath. "And now, I would have to say that I'm here because I care about you."

His words warmed her to the bone. She had never known someone willing to give up so much like Matthew had. She admired him, but did she care for him romantically? What if Dylan was alive? Wouldn't it make more sense to get back together with him for Jamie's sake?

They drove for another ten minutes not seeing anything but country roads and fields of snow. She scanned the landscape. Her concern for Jamie overrode her confusion over her feelings for Matthew. There had to be someplace where they could make a phone call. "It seems like I remember passing a gas station or house the last time we came this way." She had been in pain back then and not really paying attention, so she wasn't entirely sure.

Matthew rounded several curves. "There, I see lights."

As they approached, a gas station that was also a bait store in the summer came into view. The place looked dark, completely abandoned.

"Someone might still be here," she said. "We have to try. It'll be too late if we wait until we're in town."

He rolled to a stop, and she jumped out. She ran to the gas station and banged on the door with the Closed sign. Matthew disappeared around the corner of the gas station. She could feel her hope disintegrate each time her hand hit the glass of the door without a response.

Matthew came up beside her. "Rochelle, there's a motor home back there with lights on." He held his hand out to her, and she took it. "Let's go see."

They were in this together. He cared as much about Jamie as she did. She knew that much was true.

Matthew knocked on the door. The trailer shook from someone moving inside. The door swung open. A bald, potbellied man squinted at them. "We're closed." The man leaned in preparing to shut the door.

Matthew held the door in place. "Please, sir. We're so sorry to bother you, but it's an emergency."

Rochelle stepped forward. "My son. He could— someone is trying to hurt him." The terror of what might happen to Jamie bombarded her, and she could barely get the words out. "We just need to use your phone. That's all."

The man made an exasperated noise, threw up his arms and disappeared inside the trailer. He returned a few seconds later with a phone. "You got five minutes." The old man continued to grumble about living too close to where he worked, but she picked up on the compassion beneath the complaining.

Rochelle stood in the light and punched in the numbers. Her fingers trembled so badly she hit the wrong button. She tried again. Matthew came and stood beside her as the phone rang.

"Will Naomi be there this late?" he asked her.

"She lives there." She listened to the phone ring for the third time, and tension knotted the muscles at the back of her neck.

"Hello."

Naomi's clear, sweet voice caused Rochelle to let out the breath she'd been holding. "Naomi."

"Rochelle...what is it? You sound afraid."

"Please call the police right now. There is a man coming there, and he wants to take Jamie." Rochelle gripped the phone harder.

"I...I...don't understand."

"Please, Naomi, trust me. I don't know what he will do to get at Jamie and I am so sorry. I did not think this through. I would never put those young girls in harm's way. It's just that I felt safe there all those years ago."

"Rochelle, you don't need to explain. I'll call the police. I know a place for Jamie to hide until they get here. It's going to be okay." Naomi said goodbye and hung up.

Rochelle pulled the phone away from her ear and handed it back to the man, who retreated back into his trailer after closing the door. She gazed up at Matthew. "I hope that's enough to keep him and everyone safe."

A myriad of worries tumbled through Matthew's head, but he kept them to himself. Rochelle had enough to deal with. Snow swirled out of the sky as he touched his hand to her cheek. "I think we were in time."

"I'll feel better when I can hold Jamie in my arms."

"Me, too. Let's get in that truck and go," Matthew said.

He guessed they were about half an hour from town or more because of the snow that was coming down heavily. Either way, Elwood and the other thug had maybe a fifteen-minute head start on them. That didn't give Naomi and the police much time to work with if Elwood decided to storm in and take Jamie by force. He didn't want to think about what the outcome might be if that was the choice Elwood made.

Lost in thought as he drove, Matthew didn't even see the vehicle behind him until he felt a bump to the back of the truck.

Rochelle jerked her head around. "It looks like the truck from the cabin." Her voice filled with fear.

Matthew pressed the accelerator. How much could he push this truck on the icy roads? He could see the blaring headlights of the other truck as it gained speed and came alongside them. Matthew veered toward the shoulder when the other truck edged into their lane.

Rochelle gripped the dashboard so hard her hands turned white. Their truck swerved dangerously close to the edge of the road. Matthew straightened the wheel and tried to get ahead of the other vehicle.

"I can't go any faster," he said.

"He's coming right at us again." Rochelle spoke through gritted teeth.

"Time to play some offense." Matthew jerked the wheel, making contact with the other truck. Metal crunched and scraped. For several hundred yards it was as if the two trucks were hooked together, one dragging the other down the perilous dark road.

Rochelle took in a sharp breath and pointed through the windshield. "Car coming."

The thug's truck slowed and slipped in behind them as the oncoming car whizzed by them.

Matthew gulped in air. The headlights of the other

truck filled his rearview mirror. He gripped the steering wheel a little tighter and braced for impact.

The other truck slipped into the parallel lane but did not line up with them. Instead, the driver hit their truck bed with his front end. The back end of their truck arced out. Matthew pumped the brake and tried to get the truck under control. It swerved in a serpentine pattern and then sailed off the road. They thundered to a stop about twenty feet from the road in deep snow.

Matthew blinked several times, seeking to absorb what had happened. He glanced over at Rochelle. "You all right?"

She shook her head. "I think so."

He turned the key in the ignition. The car sputtered to life. "Can't be the same sad story every time. Here we are on this same road having another car accident. At least the truck started."

Despite the tension of the moment, Rochelle laughed. "You always see the bright side of everything."

Matthew cranked the wheel. "Let's see if we can get this thing back on the road."

"I don't see the other truck anywhere. Do you suppose he figured he did his job and sped on by?"

"Scarface wasn't crazy about killing us, but his own life is on the line if he doesn't."

Rochelle spoke under her breath. "Elwood is a piece of work."

Their truck lumbered forward through the deep snow. He couldn't see much of the road in the dark from where they were positioned.

"Are we going to be able to get back up there?"

"This hill is nothing compared to the one we rolled

down last time. I'm a little more worried about how deep the snow is," Matthew said.

The truck eased forward as Matthew scanned the dark landscape. Their windshield shattered, sending glass flying everywhere. His arm moved protectively toward Rochelle. "Get down. He's shooting at us."

Rochelle slipped down to the floor and put her arms over her head.

Matthew crouched down below the steering wheel. He could feel his blood pumping as his adrenaline kicked up a notch. Cool air came in from where the window had been broken. The bullet had hit the middle of the windshield and was probably embedded in the seat. He looked up but couldn't see the shooter anywhere. Which meant the guy must have a rifle. A handgun wouldn't have that kind of range.

He had no other choice. He had to head for the road, which kept them in the line of fire. Getting the truck back on the road was their only chance for escape. He pressed the accelerator to the floor. The truck went only slightly faster through the deep snow. Another rifle shot knocked his side mirror off. He could barely see above the dashboard.

Once they got back up to the road, they'd have to contend with the thug chasing them again, but he didn't want to leave the safety that the truck provided.

"Can you see the road?" Rochelle still had her hands over her head.

"Yeah, I see it. I don't see his truck anywhere." Judging from where the shots had come from, the shooter was in a grove of trees not far from the road. If he'd left his truck, it bought them time to get away once they got out to the road.

The motor revved and the back tires spun. He let up on the accelerator and turned the wheel to get out of the ruts he'd dug. The truck still wasn't making much progress. He glanced out the side window. The shooter had come out of the shadows and was walking toward them, preparing to take aim.

"What is it? What do you see?" Rochelle's panicked voice struck an anxious chord inside of him.

"We've got to get out of this truck. He's coming straight for us."

"But how will we get back into town?" She'd already crawled up on the seat and opened the passenger-side door.

He slipped out behind her. "We'll take his truck. We'll still have a head start on him." The darkness would provide some cover for them as they headed toward the road. He left the motor running so the shooter might think they were still in the truck.

Using the snowbanks as a shield, they ran parallel to the road until they were some distance away. They heard more shots fired at the truck, more glass shattering.

Rochelle stuttered in her step at the booming sounds of the rifle.

"Keep moving." Though his heart was racing, he managed to keep his voice calm.

They stepped out onto the road. When Matthew looked over his shoulder, the shooter was peering into the truck cab. "Get down on the other side of the road before he sees us."

Rochelle scrambled to get to the other side of the road. They ran, slowed down by the deep snow.

Matthew still didn't see any sign of the shooter's

truck. He had no way of knowing if the shooter had spotted them or finally realized they'd escaped. He just kept running, his legs burning from the exertion of moving through the snow. Rochelle slowed down, gasping for breath. He grabbed her hand.

Up ahead, he spotted the truck. "There it is. Come on, we can make it."

Both of them were out of breath by the time he yanked open the truck door. Rochelle got in on the passenger side. The keys had been left in the ignition. The truck started right up.

"Matthew." Her voice filled with terror as she pointed through the windshield.

The shooter stood in the middle of the road, aiming his rifle at them.

Matthew shifted into Reverse and backed up. One bullet hit the hood of the truck. The shooter marched toward them, preparing to take aim again. Rochelle dove down to the floor of the front seat.

Matthew drove backward. "I'm not going to be able to go anywhere unless I can get turned around." His voice was frantic.

Another shot bounced off the side of the truck. He slid the truck onto a shoulder and cranked the wheel to turn around.

"Is there another way to get into town?" Her voice filled with anguish.

"I know we're going in the opposite direction from where Jamie is, but there's nothing I can do about it. He'll shoot us if we try to go back that way."

She sat back up and stared out the window. "I know."

"Tell you what. We'll stop at that gas station and call Naomi again."

"That other truck probably still runs. He'll catch up with us if he gets it up on the road." Rochelle glanced out through the back window.

Matthew checked the rearview mirror. The thug no longer stood in the middle of the road. "I think we can spare five minutes for your peace of mind."

"Once there's some daylight, there should be more traffic on this road." The worried tone still colored her words.

"Yes, it would be safer to head back then," Matthew said. "He's not going to stand watch forever. If we can find a hiding place, we can wait him out."

The truck engine made a chugging noise.

She turned toward him. "Is something wrong?"

"I'm not sure." He stared down at the instrument panel. "We're losing oil pressure. That guy must have hit something in the engine when he shot at us."

The truck stuttered. Matthew pulled over to the side of the road just as the engine quit all together. He tried several times to restart it, but the truck made no noise at all.

Rochelle craned her neck. "Maybe he won't get that other truck back up to the road."

"It's not a chance we can take, Rochelle." Under normal circumstances, leaving the truck would have been foolhardy. But these were not normal circumstances. They were being hunted, and they were easy prey if they stayed in the truck.

"How far are we from that gas station?"

He peered out into the darkness. "Miles still," Matthew said. "I don't think it's realistic to walk back there."

She wrung her hands together. "I wish I knew what was going on with Jamie."

His placed his hand over hers. "Me, too, but we've got to focus on getting out of here...for Jamie."

"You're right," she said.

"Look around and see if there's anything we can take with us that might help us." This plan did not sit well with him. Everything he knew about surviving in wintertime conditions when stranded told him to stay in the truck.

"There's an extra coat here." Rochelle glanced into the truck bed. "It looks like there's some stuff back there." She reached underneath the seat. "I think I feel a crowbar down here."

The crowbar gave him an idea. "Rochelle, what if we waited for the guy and set a trap for him?"

"What are you talking about?"

He turned to face her, seeing the fear in her eyes. "It's the only way we're going to get back into town quickly. If we could overpower him somehow and take his truck. He'd be safe and warm in this truck until someone stopped to help him in the morning."

"It does seem like the smarter plan. I know we got away from him at the cabin, but this is harder. So far, all we have is a crowbar and he has a rifle."

"Come on, we can figure this out. This isn't about firepower. It's about being smart." He opened the door and wandered around. "We can hide back over there by those rocks."

Rochelle climbed into the bed of the truck and looked around. "That's far away. He'll see us coming toward him."

Matthew's mind raced through the possibilities. "We'll have to create some kind of distraction."

"You mean one of us is going to have to run out

first." She held up a tarp and a tangled mass of bungee cords.

"We'll figure it out, Rochelle. Toss both those things
out. We can use them. Let's hurry. He could be along
any minute."

"*If* he was able to get that truck up on the road,"
she said.

That was a big if. He knew the plan was far from
perfect. But his mind kept returning to Jamie and how
they needed to get into town as quickly as possible to
make sure he was okay.

Matthew tossed the tarp on the ground by the rocks.
Rochelle settled in beside him. He hung the extra coat
around her shoulders.

The snow swirled softly out of the night sky.

"Now what?"

Matthew took in a breath to steady his nerves. "Now
we wait."

SIXTEEN

After about ten minutes, a chill settled on Rochelle's skin and soaked through to her bones.

"He can't be much longer." Matthew draped his arm over her and held her close.

"If he comes at all." If this plan didn't work, they'd be out here until morning. And that might be too late. She was worried sick about Jamie. If only there was a way to find out if he was safe. She'd never forgive herself if anything happened to Naomi or the young girls who lived there, either. She squeezed her eyes shut, trying to block out the dark thoughts.

"This plan will work, Rochelle. It has to."

She could barely feel his body heat through the layers of clothes. She appreciated the strength of his arm around her. As a matter of fact, she appreciated everything about him. Her mind returned to the gentle kiss he'd given her earlier, completely unexpected and totally wonderful.

She struggled to envision a time when all of this would be behind her. It just didn't seem like it was possible that she and Jamie would be able to stay in

Discovery. Right now, they needed to live through the next half hour. That was as far ahead as she could see.

She stared down the road. A set of headlights appeared around a curve. Rochelle tensed as her heart pounded against her rib cage. She leaned closer to Matthew. The vehicle never slowed as it approached the parked truck. It sped past them. She stared at the red taillights glaring through the snowfall.

"That could have been our ride to someplace safe," she said.

"We had no way of knowing." He pulled her close.

Despite what they faced—a long time in the cold and a confrontation—she liked being with Matthew. She felt safe with him. He'd proved over and over that he had her back.

"I'm starting to get really cold. Maybe we should walk around a little." Matthew let go of her and pushed himself to his feet. "We can still watch the road."

She paced with her arms folded over her chest. She stopped for a moment and looked at him. She had to live this nightmare, but Matthew had volunteered for it. "I sure know how to show a guy a good time, don't I?"

He shrugged. "I'm just glad that I had any time at all with you."

Her heart warmed toward him even more. "I guess that's the best way to look at it."

Matthew turned to face her. "Maybe we'll have more time together in the future." She picked up on the vulnerability in his voice.

"Maybe. I'm not sure what Jamie and I will do if…I mean when this is all resolved." She had come to care deeply about Matthew, but the uncertainty of the next few hours overrode the positive emotions. Dylan might still be alive. Elwood might get away. She might lose Jamie forever. That thought struck like a dagger through her heart.

"I understand." His voice was saturated with disappointment.

She grabbed his hand and squeezed it. "No one should have to make the kind of sacrifices you made and not get anything in the end."

"Rochelle, if we get through this, it's reward enough to know that you and Jamie are safe."

"The more I'm with you, the more I admire you, Matthew." She tore off her glove and placed a hand on his cheek. "Maybe if we do get through this, we can do something really ordinary like go for a walk, the three of us."

He leaned toward her. "I'd like that."

"Wish I could promise more." It was the most honest thing she could say to him. She felt drawn to him in that moment, but there was no telling what the next few hours held. Would they even come out of this alive?

The glare of headlights broke the enchantment created by being close to him. They both ducked down. "I have an idea." Matthew touched her shoulder. "Go lie down in the truck. He'll see you and be distracted. I'll come up behind him and hit him with the crowbar."

She didn't question his plan. She trusted him completely. The vehicle drew even closer. She ran to the passenger side of the truck and climbed in. She saw the truck slowing right before she lay down with her feet pressed against the driver's-side door.

She prayed that Matthew had been able to move into place quickly and that the thug wouldn't notice him hiding in the shadows because he was focused on her. Her face pressed against the rough fabric of the truck seat.

She detected the roar of an engine and then the silence that followed as it was turned off. She held her breath. A truck door slammed shut. She was tempted to raise her head above the dashboard to see what was going on. What if he saw Matthew first and had attacked him? Matthew would need her help.

She brushed the thought from her mind.

Stay with the plan, Rochelle.

The door to the truck she was in clicked open. She lifted her head and turned.

Scarface grinned at her. "Look what I found here. All by yourself. Did your boyfriend go for help?"

"Please, don't hurt me." Rochelle peered over his shoulder without moving her head. She didn't see Matthew anywhere.

The thug reached in and grabbed her wrist. His rifle was slung over his shoulder. Just then Rochelle heard footsteps crunching on snow. The thug turned just as Matthew brought the crowbar down, missing his head and landing on his shoulder. The thug lunged at Matthew. Both men fell to the ground. Rochelle jumped on the thug's back, wrapping her arm around his neck while she tried to work the rifle shoulder strap free. Scarface landed a blow to Matthew's face before rising to his feet and trying to shake Rochelle off. Matthew punched the man hard in the stomach, and he doubled over. Rochelle grabbed the rifle and pointed it at the thug. "Stop right now or I'll shoot." Her voice vibrated with fear.

The thug tilted his head. "Do you even know how to use that thing, honey?"

"Is that a chance you want to take?" Her voice sounded a little stronger.

Matthew strode over to her and took the rifle. "I know how to use it. Put your hands behind your back."

Rochelle pulled the bungee cords out of her pocket and tied the man's hands behind his back. "I'm sure someone will be along to help you," she said.

Matthew pointed toward the truck. "Get in there."

"Just a second. I want to check his pockets for a phone." She found one in his coat pocket.

The thug crawled into the cab of the truck. Rochelle retrieved the extra coat she'd found and put it on Scarface's lap. "This will keep you warm."

"Why are you doing that?" The thug seemed confused by her kindness. He shook his head.

She felt a pang of guilt. This man had to go through all of this to keep from being killed by Elwood. She knew the man was probably a criminal, but still, he was a human being, too. She held up the phone. "I'll call the highway patrol and let them know where you are. You won't be out here long."

The thug's perplexed expression didn't change, but his voice softened. "Whatever, lady. You don't make any sense to me. I just tried to kill you."

She closed the truck door, feeling a bit uneasy about leaving Scarface out here by himself.

"He'll be all right, and he won't run," Matthew said. "We can't take him with us. Too much risk."

Rochelle nodded and strode toward the truck that still worked. Matthew was right. Maybe Scarface wasn't a killer, but his actions revealed how afraid of Elwood he was. He would do what he had to do to keep himself alive.

They both got in the truck. Cold air came through where the windows had been broken by rifle shots.

As Matthew pulled out onto the road, Rochelle dialed Naomi's number. With each ring, she gripped the phone a little tighter. "No one is answering."

"Give it a little more time," Matthew said. "After that, hang up and try again in a few minutes."

She picked up on the worry in his voice. She let it ring several more times before clicking it off. She stared at the phone, growing more and more fearful. "Guess I better call the highway patrol to come get Elwood's hired muscle."

After she did, Matthew took her hand. "We don't know anything about Jamie for sure yet. Let's get into town before we jump to conclusions. It's late. Naomi, Jamie and everyone could be fast asleep and safe right now."

She stared out at the dark highway ahead of them and prayed that Matthew was right.

As they neared the edge of town, Matthew struggled to let go of the images that raged through his head. He pictured all sorts of bad things happening to Jamie. Even as he'd offered Rochelle hope, he knew there was a possibility that the outcome could be bad. He cared about Jamie a lot. He didn't know what he'd do if something happened to that kid. He'd seen what an animal Elwood Corbin was.

The lights of Discovery came into view. The city sat in a valley surrounded by mountains. As the truck sped down the winding road, drawing nearer to the city limits, his stomach tightened into a hard knot.

He slowed down when he entered town, weaving

through the quiet city streets. "We could call into the police station and find out if anything happened."

"I think I'd rather go straight to Naomi's Place." She rested her face in her hands.

"Understood," Matthew said. The tension in his muscles increased the closer he got to Naomi's Place. He took the final turn and slowed down as they drew near. A police car was parked out front. He didn't know if that was a good sign or a bad sign.

"We can find out from him what happened here." Matthew spoke as gently as he could.

Rochelle crossed her arms over her body and leaned forward. "That seems like the place to start."

He'd barely pulled the truck to the curb before Rochelle jumped out and tapped on the police officer's window. Matthew came up behind her.

Officer Bryan Keyes sat behind the wheel.

Rochelle crossed her arms against the nighttime cold. "What happened here?"

"We called Naomi to warn her that Elwood was on his way," Matthew added.

Bryan said, "We had a strong police presence here as soon as we got the call, and the guy never showed up. Maybe he came by, saw all the patrol units and backed off."

Rochelle let out a heavy breath. "You mean everybody is okay?" She pressed her gloved palm to her chest.

"Safe and sound," Bryan said.

She wrapped her arms around Matthew. He relished her closeness as a sense of elation spread through him. Jamie was okay.

"We've got to get this guy. The passes are going to

be open in another ten hours. We can't watch the airport forever." Bryan leaned out of the window a little farther. "It's even more pressing now because they've identified that body in Seattle as Dylan Corben."

Rochelle let go of Matthew. "I guess that's it then." Her stillness and posture suggested a dramatic mood change.

He understood why she'd been holding out hope that Elwood had been telling the truth, and it was hard to watch her joy disappear. Still, he couldn't help but think that her letting go of Dylan would be a good thing in the end.

Bryan looked at Rochelle. "If we can catch this guy and send him back to Seattle, your testimony will put him in jail," he said.

"I'd have to face him in a courtroom." Her voice held a note of fear.

"You want him behind bars, don't you?"

"More than anything," she said.

Matthew tugged on her coat. "Let's go see Jamie."

"You'll be fine. I'll patrol the block here in a minute," said Bryan.

Matthew led the way to back of the schoolhouse. "This is all good news, right?"

"Yes," said Rochelle. Her voice sounded a little distant as though she were mulling something over. "There was a part of me that still hoped Dylan was alive."

"I know."

She turned to face him. "I know I have to let him go. It's just really hard for me."

"He's the father of your kid," Matthew said.

"I didn't realize I was holding on to his memory until I met you." She took off her glove and touched his face with her hand. "I never had a reason to let him go until now."

He leaned in and kissed her. This time, his lips lingered on hers as he wrapped his arm around her waist and drew her close. He soaked in the sweet honey scent of her neck and held her close. "This is almost over. They're going to catch Elwood and bring him to justice. You'll be able to stay here in Discovery."

She remained in his arms but pulled back a little, tilting her head to look up at him. "I can believe that now."

"Let's go see how your son is doing."

The back of Naomi's Place was darker than the front. As they climbed the steps together, Rochelle smiled and it warmed his heart.

Rochelle held her gloved hand out to knock. "I guess we'll be waking somebody up."

"It's worth it to see Jamie though, huh?"

"I can't wait to hug him," she said.

Matthew heard something rustling in the bushes surrounding the back parking lot and turned in the direction of the noise. Shadows moved toward them at a rapid pace. Elwood and his thug were on top of them before Matthew could even comprehend that it was them.

The thug wrapped his beefy arms underneath Matthew's armpits as he struggled to break free and help Rochelle, who was being dragged away by Elwood, her face filled with terror. The thug let go of Matthew but punched his head and stomach before Matthew could react. Matthew went down to his knees. He heard the thug's retreating footfalls as he pushed himself to his feet and struggled to take in a breath.

They must have been lying in wait, knowing that this was the first place Rochelle would come to when she got into town. Scarface must have phoned in that they'd escaped before he left the cabin.

Matthew scrambled to his feet. The patrol car rolled by in the alley. Matthew ran toward it and yanked open the passenger-side door. "Rochelle. They've got her. They must have a car close by."

"I'll get them," said Bryan.

"I'm going with you." Matthew jumped into the car before the detective could protest.

Bryan sped down the alley and out into the street.

Matthew heard the roar of a car engine and a moment later a car sped by.

"That has to be them," he said.

As Bryan pulled out onto the street, he picked up his radio. "This is unit twelve. I am in pursuit of Elwood Corben heading west on Seventh Street." He gave a description of the vehicle.

A female dispatcher responded. "Roger that. I'll send another unit to try and intersect the suspect."

Bryan hit the sirens. The car in front of them slowed down and pulled over.

Matthew pressed his back against the seat. What was going on here? Elwood wouldn't give up that easily. "This might be an ambush."

"We always assume it is." The headlights of the police vehicle illuminated Elwood's car as he pulled to a stop behind it. Bryan opened the car door and pulled his weapon as he approached the passenger side of the car.

"Please, open the door slowly, step out of the vehicle and lie facedown on the ground."

Matthew put his hand on the door handle, prepared to jump out and help if Bryan needed him. The car door opened, and a man who clearly wasn't Elwood or the thug got out.

Matthew clenched his teeth. They'd lost their chance to save Rochelle.

SEVENTEEN

Rochelle's cheek pressed against the carpet of the back of the SUV where she'd been tossed. Elwood and his thug had been in a hurry and hadn't had time to restrain her in any way. Every time she lifted her head, though, the thug turned around and pointed a gun at her.

"We'll wait here for a couple of minutes," said Elwood. "That cop's going to be looking for a car trying to get away."

The minutes ticked by. Rochelle bent her head and stared at the backseat door of the SUV. Elwood had clicked the locks. There was no way she could get away even though she was only a block or so from Naomi's Place.

A siren sounded in the distance and grew fainter. Elwood's plan had worked. Her hope of rescue was carried away with the fading siren.

"We're in the clear." Elwood chuckled as he started the car and pulled out of the alley. "Where are we supposed to go to get this done? We need some place isolated. The snowstorm limits our options."

"Back to the cabin," said the thug.

"What are you, dumb, Ralph? You don't think they

figured out by now we rented that place?" Elwood sounded irritated. "All those police around that baby factory. I'm sure they've figured out a lot about me. I've spent too much time in this town. This was supposed to be quick."

They rolled forward on the silent, dark street.

After a long pause, Ralph spoke up. "There's got to be an open field around here somewhere or some trees or something."

Elwood didn't answer right away. He must be mulling over the possibilities for where to kill her. Rochelle counted the seconds before Elwood said something. "Not an open field but that new construction I saw off of Box Elder Street. This time of night there won't be anyone there. Probably a hole we can toss the body into." Elwood took a sharp turn, and Rochelle slammed against the side of the car.

Elwood's words made her breath catch in her throat. This was it then. After such a long fight, Elwood would win anyway. Jamie's face, the sound of his laughter, flashed through her mind. And then Matthew's face and the gentle quality of his voice entered her mind. Not seeing him again hurt almost as much as the thought of being separated from Jamie. Her heart was finally open to loving him and now it would never happen. She said a feverish prayer.

Oh, God, what are You doing here? How can it be my life is ending when it just seems to be coming together?

Rochelle's hands were shaking when she touched them to her face. The case against Elwood would fall apart without her eyewitness testimony. If Elwood didn't go to jail, he'd find some other way to get to Jamie. If he wasn't ever caught for killing her, he might find some legal means to get custody of her son. But Matthew knew the whole truth about Elwood and had seen some of it firsthand. He would fight to protect Jamie from that kind of evil.

Matthew cared about Jamie as much as she did. Maybe if their lives had played out differently, the three of them could have been together. Her affection for him had been too little too late.

The car swayed back and forth on the road. She wasn't afraid to die, to be with her Savior. What she felt was deep sorrow over missing out on seeing Jamie grow up and wondering if there could have been something between her and Matthew.

The car slowed down. They must be close to their destination.

"We need to find someplace they won't find her for a long time…maybe not ever." Elwood's voice cut through to her bones.

She shivered. There had to be justice for all Elwood had done. Maybe he wouldn't go to jail for what he'd done to Dylan, but Officer Keyes and Matthew knew what Elwood's intentions were even if they didn't find her body.

"How about back over there?" said Ralph.

"That might work. Get out. Look around for a hole we can throw some dirt on after we drop the body in there, something that will be totally covered eventually," Elwood said. The car jolted to a stop, and a door opened and slammed shut.

The air seemed to get heavier now that she knew she was alone in the car with Elwood.

She lifted her head up and stared at the back of his

head. Trying to talk him out of this would be a pointless waste of breath.

"Don't say I didn't give you enough chances, Rochelle." Elwood didn't turn to look at her as he spoke.

Rage smoldered inside her. What a sociopath. She'd seen one or two of his type in the courtroom. His view of the world was so twisted. Nothing was ever his fault. From Elwood's point of view he was compelled to kill her because she hadn't done what he wanted.

Ralph came and tapped on Elwood's window. "I think I found the place, boss."

"Good, get her out of here." The back door of the car opened and the thug motioned with his gun. "Come on."

She crawled out. A chill hung in the night air. When she looked up at the sky, she thought it was the most beautiful thing she'd ever seen. The stars twinkled down at her. Gossamer clouds drifted past the half-moon. The beauty of the night sky inspired her not to give up. She glanced around as Ralph pushed her forward. There had to be a way to escape. She wanted to live to see that justice was done where Elwood Corben was concerned. She wanted to hug Jamie and Matthew again.

She knew this place. It'd been in the news. They were in a subdivision where construction had been shut down when the owner ran out of money. She could see the skeletal frames of two houses up ahead. She looked over her shoulder. Elwood had remained behind. Of course, he wouldn't get his hands dirty. She was pretty sure, though, that he had a gun. She heard Elwood's phone ring just as they started walking away.

"Where are you taking me?" Maybe she could distract Ralph long enough to run away.

He pressed the gun in her back. "Keep moving."

He led her by the second unfinished house. They stepped past a piece of earth-moving equipment next to a large hole.

"You're going to throw me in there?"

"And bury you. Just enough dirt to cover you up. In the spring, I'm sure this hole will be filled in." The thug seemed to take pleasure in telling her that. "Now walk toward the edge of that hole and turn your back to me."

Bryan Keyes took the phone away from his ear. "Looks like we caught a break."

Matthew's chest had felt as if it was in a vise ever since they'd stopped the wrong car. They'd been patrolling the streets and listening to the radio to see if the other patrol car caught any sign of Elwood's SUV.

"What are you talking about?" he asked.

Bryan started the patrol car and pulled out of the parking lot where they'd stopped. "That thug you left for the highway patrol to pick up had a real change of heart. He was moved by Rochelle's kindness. First thing he did when he was picked up was say he wanted to take Elwood down. He just phoned Elwood to say he was back to help and Elwood gave up his location to him. He's over in the Brentwood subdivision off Box Elder. Units are on their way over."

Matthew's heart skipped a beat. "Then that's where we need to be."

Rochelle stared down into the dark hole and closed her eyes.

"Hey, what's going on here?" Ralph said.

Rochelle turned to where Ralph was looking. Elwood

ran toward them. She heard sirens in the distance. This time they were growing louder instead of fading.

Elwood grabbed her and yanked her toward the SUV "You're coming with me."

"Don't leave me high and dry," said Ralph, running after them.

Elwood pointed a gun at Ralph. "You get out of here."

Ralph raised his hand and backed away. "I see how you are."

Two patrol cars with flashing lights came down parallel streets. Ralph sprinted off into the darkness as Elwood shoved Rochelle in front of himself, using her as a shield while he put the gun to her head.

One of the patrol cars chased after Ralph while the other came toward Elwood. Bryan Keyes got out of the car and pulled his gun.

"You come toward me and she dies," said Elwood.

He pressed the gun harder against her temple. Her pulse drummed in her ears as her breath came in shallow gasps.

The passenger-side door of the patrol car opened up, and Matthew stepped out, shielding himself behind the door. In the darkness, she couldn't make out his expression. She wondered then if this was the last time she would ever see him.

"Come on, Elwood, you don't want it to end this way." Bryan's voice was unwavering.

Elwood dragged Rochelle backward toward his SUV. With the gun still pointed at her, Elwood said to her, "Open the door."

Her hand trembled as she reached for the door handle.

"Get in and scoot over to the driver's side," Elwood

said to her and then shouted at the men. "I still have the gun on her, so don't try anything. If you follow me, she dies on the spot."

She didn't dare look behind her to see what Officer Keyes was doing.

Elwood smashed the keys into her hand. "Now drive." He pressed the gun against her stomach. "Fast."

She started the car and pulled out onto the road. "Where do you want me to go?"

"Take the fastest way out of town," Elwood said.

"The passes are closed." She checked the rearview mirror when Elwood turned toward the side window, just a quick glance. The patrol car was not behind them, but certainly they would find a way to follow her.

Elwood raised his voice and poked the gun in her side. "Take me someplace where a helicopter can land."

As her heart pounded against her rib cage, she was having trouble forming a thought or remembering the layout of the town. They sped past several fields covered in snow and a farmhouse set back from the road.

"I guess the road to the ski hill would be the closest. They plow that one pretty fast." She hit the blinker and took a turn. What were Bryan and Matthew doing? Maybe they were hanging back thinking that would keep her from getting killed right away. Maybe they would get another patrol unit to intersect with them. They must know Elwood planned to kill her no matter what. This move only bought her a little time.

The houses and barns grew farther apart as she drove down the two-lane road.

"What is that place?" Elwood pointed to a sign that read Fish Technology Center. "Are there people there in the winter?"

She'd gone there on a field trip with Jamie at the beginning of the school year. "I think it's pretty much shut down." She wasn't sure about that. Her hope was that there was a park ranger watching the place.

"Pull in there then." Elwood pointed with his gun.

She hit her blinker a long time before the turn, hoping that if the patrol car was far behind them, they'd see where she went and not speed past. They rolled down a snow-packed road and into a parking lot. Though the lot had been plowed, there were no other cars. She saw no sign of life anywhere. Several of the buildings had exterior lights on, but they were probably automatic. Someone might be here during the day, but it looked as if the place was abandoned at this hour.

"Now give me the keys." He pushed the gun against her shoulder and held out his hand. "I'm going to get out first. Don't you move until I'm standing outside your door."

"Elwood, they are going to know that you killed me."

Elwood lifted his chin defiantly. "They're not going to find your body and they're not going to find me. I have enough resources and connections to disappear into any country I want. Shame to give up the business, but I can start over and rebuild. Should have done that right after you left town ten years ago. Guess I was just too attached to my life in Seattle. Besides, I thought my tracks were covered for good."

"They're watching the airport." She felt she was grasping at straws, but she had to do something to slow him down.

"That is a minor technicality. I can charter a private plane under a different name." Elwood let out a huff of air. "You forget, sweetheart. I've been in this game a long time." He pulled out his phone and dialed a number. She listened while Elwood ordered a helicopter to come to get him. "Yeah, ten minutes should do it." He hung up and glanced at her. "That, my dear, is the power that I have. Now, get moving."

He pushed her past what looked like series of small iced-over swimming pools where the fish were stored in warmer weather.

She slowed her walk. How thick was the ice on that water?

"Hurry." Elwood nudged her.

"I'm going as fast as I can. It's kind of narrow here and icy." She stared down at the pool. If she miscalculated, he might have time to shoot her. It was a chance she was willing to take. She whirled around, slamming her elbow into Elwood's stomach and knocking him sideways.

Elwood stumbled and lost his grip on the gun as he fell. As he did, his body hit the icy pool and broke through. He screamed.

She sprinted toward one of the larger buildings. She'd seen him put the SUV keys in his pocket so there was no chance of escape that way.

Bryan and Matthew had to be on their way. All she had to do was hold Elwood off. She heard him cursing behind her as her feet pounded through the snow. The first building was locked.

When she glanced over her shoulder, Elwood was crawling out of the pool and looking for his gun. She ran toward a larger building around the back. They'd gone through this building on the field trip. The ranger had commented on the lock needing to be replaced. When she tried the door it slid open. Except for some lights over the fish tanks the room was dark. The warm temperature of the room suggested that fish were kept here in the winter. She walked past a round container where trout were swimming.

She slipped behind one of the fish vats in a dark corner. Her heart was still pounding. Chances were good that Elwood had seen her run this way. She kept her ears tuned for his footfalls, even as she heard water gurgling and dripping from somewhere. She had pressed lower into the darkness of the corner when she heard the door creak open.

Rochelle held her breath. A single light clicked on and Elwood's footsteps pounded on the concrete. "Rochelle, I know you're in here."

The sinister tone of his voice cut through her to the bone.

She prayed Bryan and Matthew got here in time, before Elwood found her.

EIGHTEEN

Matthew stared out at the dark road ahead. "There, they turned there." He'd seen only a momentary blinking, but it had to be them.

"Are you sure?" Bryan squinted as they whizzed past the Fish Technology Center sign.

"Yes, I'm sure. The turnoff is coming up." It had been risky to hang back when Elwood had taken off with Rochelle. Bryan had reasoned that if they raced after Rochelle, Elwood would keep his word and shoot her on the spot. Hanging back gave her a fighting chance, but it also made it harder to keep track of Elwood.

Bryan rolled the patrol car down the road. A single vehicle sat parked in the lot.

"Good call," said Bryan.

They got out of the patrol car as lights clicked on in a far building.

"That must be where they are." Bryan pulled his gun. "Maybe you should hang back."

He nodded, and Bryan took off toward the building. Matthew had no intention of standing here doing nothing. He wasn't about to let Rochelle die when he had the power to stop it. He knew Bryan was only following protocol where civilians were concerned. But this was Rochelle's life they were talking about. The woman he loved.

He skirted around the building in the opposite direction that Bryan had gone. When he peered through a dusty window, he saw Elwood taking aim at Bryan as the police officer slipped through an open door. Bryan dove toward the ground just as the shot was fired. Matthew wasn't sure if Bryan had been hit or not. Bryan took cover behind a piece of metal equipment…or maybe he was lying there bleeding.

Elwood stalked toward a dark corner of the room, reached down and jerked Rochelle to her feet. Matthew's heart squeezed tight. He raced around to the building to the open door.

Outside he heard the sound of a helicopter. That had to be something Elwood had ordered. By the time he burst across the threshold, Elwood and Rochelle were gone. Bryan Keyes lay on the floor clutching his leg.

"You all right?"

"I'll make it," Bryan spoke through gritted teeth. He pointed to where his gun had slid across the floor. "Go get them."

Matthew picked up the gun and ran.

The sound of the helicopter grew more and more oppressive as Elwood dragged Rochelle toward it. The gun jabbed deeper into her side when he swung around to look back at the building. He must think someone was still going to come after him.

Elwood had shot either Bryan or Matthew. She wasn't sure who. Nor did she know if the person was dead or alive. She had to find a way to get away from Elwood before he ended her life.

The helicopter touched down in an open area. The chopper blades created an intense wind and a mechanical hum that seemed to swallow up everything else.

"You're free as a bird, Elwood. What do you need with me?" she shouted to be heard.

"You, my dear, are a loose end." He pushed her forward. From the way he kept looking over his shoulder, Elwood clearly believed that either Matthew or Bryan would come for him.

So Elwood would use her as a shield to get on the helicopter and keep her rescuers at bay, but in the end he would shoot her anyway. As usual, Elwood had rigged the game.

A deep male voice boomed off to one side. "I don't think so, Elwood."

She heard a thud and Elwood let go of her. She whirled around to see Matthew standing there holding the barrel of a gun. He'd hit Elwood with the handle. Stunned, Elwood took a step back. It took him a moment to raise his gun and point it at Matthew. The hesitation allowed Matthew time to dive toward him. Matthew grabbed Elwood's wrist that held the gun and twisted it. The gun fell into the snow.

Elwood took a swipe at Matthew, but Matthew dodged him. Sirens sounded in the distance as Matthew landed a blow across Elwood's jaw. Elwood dove for Matthew, and the two men rolled around in the snow as the sirens grew louder. Elwood ended up on top of Matthew, hitting him over and over.

"Stop it," Rochelle yelled, and pushed Elwood.

Elwood turned his anger on her and dove toward her

as she screamed. He was on top of her, punching her. Matthew still lay in the snow, incapacitated.

The helicopter lifted a few feet off the ground. The pilot must not have wanted to stick around for the trouble he saw brewing. Alert to the situation, Elwood jumped to his feet and ran toward the helicopter.

The pilot brought the chopper back down to the ground.

"He's getting away." Rochelle's words seemed to fall three feet in front of her.

But Matthew must have heard her, because he raced toward Elwood. Now that his back was against the wall, Elwood had given up on killing her and instead was focused on escape. If they didn't catch him now, he'd simply disappear and set himself up somewhere else in the world to do the same kind of evil he'd done all along.

Flashing lights came into view as several patrol cars rolled down the road toward the parking lot. At the same time Matthew closed in on Elwood. Rochelle trailed after him. Matthew leaped into the air in an attempt to bring Elwood down to the ground. Elwood managed to throw him off and continued to run toward the waiting helicopter.

Rochelle ran past where Matthew was getting to his feet. She leaped forward and grabbed hold of Elwood's leg. This man had been the source of her anxious thoughts and concern for Jamie's future for too long. She wasn't about to let him get away.

Elwood struggled to free himself, but she held on. Matthew caught up with them just as the helicopter lifted off the ground. He leaped up and grasped Elwood's other leg. When Elwood fell down to the ground, Rochelle was still holding on to him.

At least half a dozen police officers made their way toward them as the helicopter lifted off and disappeared into the night sky…without Elwood Corben. Elwood still wrestled as Matthew held him down.

Rochelle finally let go of Elwood's leg. "Thanks for your help. I couldn't have done it without you."

"Yeah, we make a pretty good team." Though his focus was on restraining Elwood, Rochelle picked up on the adoration in his voice.

The police officers made their way toward them. As they hauled Elwood away, Rochelle glanced back toward the building where Bryan had emerged, limping but making his way toward them.

Rochelle let out a breath. "He made it."

Within minutes, Elwood was in a squad car and an ambulance was talking Bryan to the hospital.

One of the other officers approached Rochelle and Matthew. "Could you folks use a ride into town?"

"Yes," said Matthew. "We need to go see her son." He wrapped his arms around her.

The ride into town was almost surreal. The sun came up over the horizon turning the sky pink. As they approached Naomi's Place, Rochelle felt a lightness that had been ten years in coming. And none of this would have happened if Matthew hadn't chosen to be so unselfish.

From the back of the patrol car where they both sat, she turned to face him.

He raised an eyebrow. "What?"

She placed her hand on his chest. "I was just thinking what a great neighbor I have. And how I am so looking forward to getting to know him better."

He pressed his forehead against hers. "Under less trying circumstances."

"Yes." She felt a rush of deep affection for him. She touched his cheek. More than affection, she thought. Love. Yes, she was sure of it. She'd never known anyone as wonderful as Matthew.

When the patrol car pulled up to Naomi's Place, Jamie was at the window looking out. He ran to greet them. Rochelle took her son in her arms as Matthew's arm wrapped around both of them.

"I'm so glad to see you guys," said Jamie.

"Me, too, little buddy," said Matthew.

They pulled free of the hug slowly, all three of them staring at each other.

"So everything is okay now?" said Jamie. "The bad man won't hurt us."

Rochelle touched his soft hair. "No, he won't hurt us ever again."

"And we can stay in our old house?"

"Yes."

"And Matthew can come over and have hot cocoa with us and make a snowman in the backyard?"

"I'd like that." Matthew held Rochelle in his gaze.

She saw the look in his eyes. It was something more than affection. He felt it, too. "Yes, that would be a good place to start."

The three of them embraced.

As they walked toward the converted schoolhouse that had given her and her son a fighting chance, Jamie slipped in between them and held both of their hands. "You two should just get married," he said.

Matthew glanced over at her, amusement dancing in his eyes. "Why is that, Jamie?"

She felt the rush of warmth through her that his attention created.

"It would just be easier for all of us," he said matter-of-factly. "He's going to be over at the house all the time anyway."

Both of them laughed.

"You might be right about that," she said. She tried to picture her life sometime in the future. Jamie, Matthew and her hanging out doing something incredibly normal like watching a movie.

"I couldn't agree with you more, Jamie," said Matthew. He gave Rochelle's hand a squeeze, and she wondered if there might be an engagement in the future.

EPILOGUE

Naomi looked festive in her blue velvet dress when she opened the door for Matthew, Rochelle and Jamie. "I'm so glad you could make it a little early before the party starts. The others are waiting in the lounge." She leaned forward as they came up the back steps. "Jamie, it's so good to see you again."

She led them down the hall. The entire lounge was decorated for Christmas. Rochelle's heart skipped a beat when she saw her friends from ten years ago. Sarah stood off to the side holding Bryan's hand. A pair of crutches was propped against the wall. Because they'd both stayed in Discovery, she'd run into Sarah from time to time, but her other good friend from that time ten years ago, Clarissa, had fallen off the face of the earth after she'd miscarried and left Naomi's Place.

She rushed over to the petite blonde and embraced her. "Clarissa." A tall man with a five-o'clock shadow stood behind her. "I thought about you so often after you disappeared."

"It's a long story but I came back to Discovery." She turned toward the man behind her. "And I'm staying here for good. This is my fiancé, Ezra Jefferson."

Ezra came forward and shook Rochelle's hand. "Clarissa told me how much the friendship with you two meant."

"How wonderful. So you're engaged, too," Rochelle said.

Clarissa turned toward Ezra. "Like I said, it's a long story, but it has a happy ending."

Sarah let go of Bryan's hand. "Naomi, could you take a picture of us?"

"Sure." Naomi wandered over to the piano and picked up a camera. "Just you three and then maybe we can get a picture of you with the four men in your lives, as well." She clicked the button. "Okay, now let's get Jamie in the front and the men in the back."

Matthew came up behind Rochelle, placing his hand on her back. She was happy for Clarissa and Sarah. Both of them would be getting married soon.

The other guests arrived, people who had supported the home over the years, along with several other women who had stayed here over that Christmas ten years ago. One of the teen girls sat down at the piano and another got out her violin to play Christmas music.

Matthew tapped her on the shoulder. "Can I talk to you for a moment?"

He took her hand and, after grabbing her coat from the rack by the door, led her outside where the snow was softly falling and the streetlight illuminated the back parking lot.

She crossed her arms over her chest. "We can't stay out here very long. It's cold." He wrapped her coat around her shoulders.

"I just wanted a moment alone with you."

She tilted her head. "Because?" She slipped into her coat.

"I thought about doing some big showy thing in front of everyone, but that's just not me. This moment is for the two of us alone."

Her heart fluttered. "Oh, Matthew."

He reached into her coat pocket and pulled out a tiny box. He winked at her. "I had Jamie slip this in your pocket earlier."

Rochelle smiled coyly. "Oh, so he knows."

"It was his idea, don't you remember?" Matthew clicked open the box to reveal a simple gold band with a single diamond. "Rochelle, will you marry me?"

"Say yes, Mom."

Rochelle glanced over to the steps where Jamie stood along with Clarissa, Ezra, Bryan and Sarah.

She gazed into the deep brown eyes of the man she wanted to spend the rest of her life with. "Yes, Matthew. I will marry you."

A cheer rose up from the steps as Matthew leaned in to kiss Rochelle.

* * * * *

Dear Reader,

I hope you enjoyed following Rochelle, Matthew and Jamie on their exciting and dangerous adventure. Rochelle faces many obstacles in finding justice against Elwood Corben. Most of us will never have to go through an ordeal like Rochelle did, but all of us have found ourselves in a David-and-Goliath battle. We have all confronted a challenge where it looked like we couldn't win and we chose to fight the battle anyway.

I recently had my own David-and-Goliath war. I decided to lose weight after many failures and years of being obese. I made my goal and lost seventy-five pounds. What was different this time? With my husband's health failing, I was more motivated to be around for our children and future grandchildren. Also, I enlisted the help and encouragement of friends and a personal trainer. Before, I used to think losing weight was all up to me. The truth is no one can fight these battles alone. We all need cheerleaders in our life. Just like Matthew and Naomi were for Rochelle, we all need to find people who help us conquer the Goliaths in our lives.

Sharon Dunn

Questions for Discussion

1. What events led Rochelle to run away when she was a teenager?

2. What has Rochelle overcome to establish a life for herself and her son?

3. Why does Rochelle think she can't go to the Discovery police for help?

4. What happened to Matthew that makes him vow to listen to his gut instinct?

5. What character qualities make Matthew a good paramedic? Do those same qualities sometimes work against him?

6. What is the turning point for Rochelle when she decides to stop running and bring Elwood to justice?

7. What things do Jamie and Matthew do together that help them bond?

8. Why does Matthew feel a connection to Jamie and want to help him have a good childhood?

9. What does Elwood say to Rochelle that makes her doubt her own memory of the night she ran away?

10. Why does Elwood want to see Jamie?

11. What kind of ordinary fun things do Jamie, Matthew and Rochelle do together despite the danger they face?

12. What was the most exciting scene for you in the book?

13. What did you think when Officer Keyes didn't show up for the meeting? Did you still trust him or not?

14. Have you ever faced a challenge like Rochelle and Matthew did, something that felt like a David-and-Goliath battle that you couldn't win?

15. How important was it that Matthew not only love Rochelle, but also Jamie?

REQUEST YOUR FREE BOOKS!
2 FREE RIVETING INSPIRATIONAL NOVELS
PLUS 2 FREE MYSTERY GIFTS

YES! Please send me 2 FREE Love Inspired® Suspense novels and my 2 FREE mystery gifts (gifts are worth about $10). After receiving them, if I don't wish to receive any more books, I can return the shipping statement marked "cancel." If I don't cancel, I will receive 4 brand-new novels every month and be billed just $4.74 per book in the U.S. or $5.24 per book in Canada. That's a savings of at least 21% off the cover price. It's quite a bargain! Shipping and handling is just 50¢ per book in the U.S. and 75¢ per book in Canada.* I understand that accepting the 2 free books and gifts places me under no obligation to buy anything. I can always return a shipment and cancel at any time. Even if I never buy another book, the two free books and gifts are mine to keep forever.

123/323 IDN F5AC

Name	(PLEASE PRINT)	
Address		Apt. #
City	State/Prov.	Zip/Postal Code

Signature (if under 18, a parent or guardian must sign)

Mail to the Harlequin® Reader Service:
IN U.S.A.: P.O. Box 1867, Buffalo, NY 14240-1867
IN CANADA: P.O. Box 609, Fort Erie, Ontario L2A 5X3

**Are you a current subscriber to Love Inspired Suspense books
and want to receive the larger-print edition?
Call 1-800-873-8635 or visit www.ReaderService.com.**

LIS13R

SPECIAL EXCERPT FROM

Love Inspired®
SUSPENSE

*SWAT team member Isaac Morrison didn't plan to
fall for his best friend's sister. But when Leah Nichols
and her son are in trouble, he'll stop at nothing to
keep them out of harm's way.*

Read on for a sneak peek of
UNDER THE LAWMAN'S PROTECTION
by Laura Scott

"Stay down. I'm going to go make sure there isn't some-one out there."

"Wait!" Leah cried as Isaac was about to open his car door. "Don't go. Stay here with us."

He was torn between two impossible choices. If some-one had shot out the tires on purpose, he couldn't just wait for that person to come finish them off. Nor did he want to leave Leah and Ben here alone.

So far he wasn't doing the greatest job of keeping Hawk's sister and her son safe. If he'd been wearing his bulletproof gear he would be in better shape to go out to investigate.

Isaac peered out the window, trying to see if anyone was out there. Sitting here was making him crazy, so he decided doing something was better than nothing.

"I'm armed, Leah, so don't worry about me. I promise I'll do whatever it takes to keep you and Ben safe."

He could tell she wanted to protest, but she bit her lip and nodded. She pulled her son out of his booster seat and tucked him next to her so that he was protected on either side. Then she curled her body around him. The fact that she would risk herself to protect Ben gave Isaac a funny feeling in the center of his chest.

Leah's actions were humbling. He hadn't been attracted to a woman in a long time, not since his wife had left him.

But this wasn't the time to ruminate over the past. Isaac's ex-wife and son were gone, and nothing in the world would bring them back. So Isaac would do the next best thing—protect Leah and Ben with his life if necessary.

Don't miss
UNDER THE LAWMAN'S PROTECTION
by Laura Scott,
available January 2015 wherever
Love Inspired® Suspense books and ebooks are sold.

As a widower, Sheriff Colt Garrett has his hands full with a rambunctious son and daughter. Could feisty schoolteacher Allison Grainger be the missing piece in their little family?

Enjoy this sneak peek at Penny Richards's
WOLF CREEK FATHER!

"I think she likes you," Brady offered.

Really? Colt thought with a start. Brady thought Allie liked him? "I like her, too." And he did, despite their on-again, off-again sparring the past year.

"Are you taking her some ice for her ice cream?" Cilla asked.

"I don't know. It depends." On the one hand, after not seeing her all week, he was anxious to see her; on the other, he wasn't certain what he would say or do when he did.

"On what?"

"A lot of things."

"But we will see her at the ice cream social, won't we?"

Fed up with the game of Twenty Questions, Colt, fork in one hand, knife in the other, rested his forearms on the edge of the table and looked from one of his children to the other. The innocence on their faces didn't fool him for a minute. What was this all about, anyway?

The answer came out of nowhere, slamming into him with the force of Ed Rawlings's angry bull when he'd pinned Colt against a fence. He knew exactly what was up.

"The two of you wouldn't be trying to push me and

Allison into spending more time together, would you?"

Brady looked at Cilla, the expression in his eyes begging her to spit it out. "Well, actually," she said, "Brady and I have talked about it, and we think it would be swell if you started courting her."

Glowering at his sister, and swinging that frowning gaze to Colt, Brady said, "What she really means is that since we have to have a stepmother, we'd like her."

"What did you say?" Colt asked, uncertain that he'd heard correctly.

"Cilla and I want Miss Grainger to be our ma."

Don't miss WOLF CREEK FATHER
by Penny Richards,
available January 2015 wherever
Love Inspired® Historical books and ebooks are sold.